"Found What You're Looking For?"

Hunter asked, leaning one big hand on the table beside her and resting the other on the back of her chair. His cheek brushed hers, and he felt her jump. His own breath caught.

He wanted her.

He wanted to grind his mouth into her own and make her cry out her need for him.

She was feeling the same tension. "You startled me," Jennifer said breathlessly.

He knew better. His lean, warm cheek touched hers. She glanced up and saw the thick, short lashes over his dark eyes, the faint lines in his cream-smooth tan. "Hunter..." His name was a soft whisper that broke involuntarily from her throat.

He turned his head, and his eyes looked deeply into hers. She could taste his breath on her mouth, smell the clean scent of his body, feel the impact of his bare arms, his chest. He intoxicated her with his nearness, as she saw the hot glitter of awareness in those black eyes.

Then she saw the dark lashes lower as his gaze dropped with fierce intent to her parted lips.

Dear Reader:

Welcome to the world of Silhouette Desire. Join me as we travel to a land of incredible passion and tantalizing romance—a place where dreams can, and do, come true.

When I read a Silhouette Desire, I sometimes feel as if I'm going on a little vacation. I can relax, put my feet up, and become transported to a new world...a world that has, naturally, a perfect hero just waiting to whisk me away! These are stories to remember, containing moments to treasure.

Silhouette Desire novels are romantic love stories—sensuous yet emotional. As a reader, you not only see the hero and heroine fall in love, you also feel what they're feeling.

In upcoming months look for books by some of your favorite Silhouette Desire authors: Joan Hohl, Ann Major, Elizabeth Lowell and Linda Lael Miller.

So enjoy!

Lucia Macro
Senior Editor

DIANA PALMER

HUNTER

SILHOUETTE *Desire*®

Published by Silhouette Books New York

America's Publisher of Contemporary Romance

SILHOUETTE BOOKS
300 East 42nd St., New York, N.Y. 10017

ISBN: 0-373-05606-0

First Silhouette Books printing November 1990

Printed in the U.S.A.

Books by Diana Palmer

DIANA PALMER

is a prolific romance writer who got her start as a newspaper reporter. Accustomed to the daily dead-lines of a journalist, she has no problem with writer's block. In fact, she averages a book every two months. Mother of a young son, Diana met and married her husband within one week: "It was just like something from one of my books."

For Flo in Canada
and Ophelia in Augusta, GA.
with love

One

___

The silver-haired man across the desk had both hands clasped together on its surface, and his blue eyes were narrow and determined.

Hunter wanted to argue. He'd protested assignments before, and Eugene Ritter had backed down. This time the old man wouldn't. Hunter sensed Ritter's determination before he even tried to get out of the job.

That didn't stop him, of course. Phillip Hunter was used to confrontation. As chief of internal security for Ritter Oil Corporation for the past ten years, he'd become quite accustomed to facing off against all manner of opponents, from would-be thieves to enemy agents who tried to get the jump on Ritter's strategic metal discoveries.

"The desert is no place for a woman," he told the old man. He sat back comfortably in the straight-backed chair, looking as formidable as his Apache ancestors. He was very dark, with jet-black hair conventionally cut, and eyes almost black in a lean, thin-lipped face. He was tall, too, and muscular. Even his perfectly fitted gray suit didn't hide the hard lines of a body kept fit by hours of exercise. Hunter was ex-Green Beret, ex-mercenary, and for a short time he'd even worked for the CIA. He was an expert with small arms and his karate training had earned him a black belt. He was thirty-seven, a loner by nature, unmarried and apt to stay that way. He had no inclination to accompany Eugene's sexy field geologist out to Arizona on a preliminary survey. Jennifer Marist was one of his few ongoing irritations. She seemed to stay in hot water, and he was always deputized to pull her irons out of the fire.

Her last exploration had put her in danger from enemy agents, resulting in a stakeout at her apartment a few months ago. Two men had been apprehended, but the third was still at large.

Hunter and Jennifer were old sparring partners. They'd been thrown together on assignments more often than Hunter liked. Like two rocks striking, they made sparks fly, and that could be dangerous. He didn't like white women, and Jennifer was unique. Her soft blond beauty, added to her sharp intellect, made him jittery. She was the only female who'd ever had that effect on him, and he didn't like it. The thought of spending a week in the desert alone with her had him fuming.

"Jennifer isn't just a woman, she's one of my top field geologists," Eugene replied. "This is a potentially rich strike, and I need the new capital it will bring in. Jennifer can't go alone."

"I could send one of my operatives with her," Hunter replied.

"Not good enough. Jennifer's already been in danger from this assignment once. I want the best—and that's you."

"We don't get along, haven't you noticed?" he said through his teeth.

"You don't have to get along with her. You just have to keep anyone from getting his hands on her maps or her survey results." He pursed his lips. "The site's in Arizona, near the Apache reservation. You can go see your grandfather."

"I can do that without having to follow your misplaced ingenue around," he said coldly.

"Jennifer is a geologist," the older man reminded him. "Her looks have nothing to do with her profession. For God's sake, you get along with my other female employees, why not with Jennifer?"

That was a question Hunter didn't really want to answer. He couldn't very well tell Eugene that the woman appealed to his senses so potently that it was hard to function when she was around. He wasn't in the market for an affair, but he wanted Jennifer with a feverish passion. He'd managed to contain his desire for her very well over the years, but lately it was becoming unmanageable. The temptation of being out on the desert with her was too much. Something might happen, and what then? He had good reasons for his dislike of white women, and he had no desire whatsoever to create a child who, like himself, could barely adapt to life in a white world. White and Apache just didn't mix, even if he did frequently wake up sweating from his vivid dreams about Jennifer Marist.

"You can always threaten to quit," Eugene advised with a sharp grin.

"Would it work?" Hunter queried.

Eugene just shook his head.

"In that case," Hunter said, rising to his feet with the stealthy grace that was unique to him, "I won't bother. When do we leave?"

"First thing in the morning. You can pick up the tickets and motel voucher from my secretary. You'll need time to lay in some camping equipment, so the motel room will be necessary the first night. You and Jennifer will be pretending to be husband and wife when you switch flights in Phoenix to head down to Tucson. That's going to throw any followers off the track, I hope, and give you both time to scout the area before they discover their mistake and double back. Better get in touch with our operatives in Arizona and advise them of the plan."

"I'll do that now."

"Try not to look so dismal, will you?" Eugene muttered darkly. "It's demoralizing!"

"Stop sending me out with Jennifer Marist."

"You're the only man in my corporation who could complain about that."

"I'm Apache," Hunter said with quiet pride. "She's white."

Eugene had been married twice and he wasn't stupid. He could read between the lines very well. "I understand how it is," he replied. "But this is business. You'll have to cope."

"Don't I always?" Hunter murmured. "Will you tell her, or do you want me to?"

"I'll enjoy it more than you would," Eugene chuckled. "She's going to go right through the ceiling. It may shock you to know that she finds you offensive and unpleasant. She'll fight as hard to get out of it as you just did."

That didn't surprise Hunter. He had a feeling Jennifer felt the same unwanted attraction he did and was fighting it just as hard. From day one, their relationship had been uneasy and antagonistic.

"It won't do her any more good than it did me," Hunter murmured. "But if she ends up roasting over a campfire, don't say I didn't warn you."

Eugene's blue eyes twinkled. "Okay. I won't."

Hunter left and walked along the corridor with an expression so cold and so fierce that one employee turned and went back the other way to avoid him. He had a fairly decent working relationship with some of Eugene's people, but most of them kept out of his way. The icy Mr. Hunter was well-known. He was the only bachelor who didn't have to fight off feminine advances. The women were too intimidated by him. All except for Jennifer, who fought him tooth and nail.

And now a week on the desert with her, he mused. He lit a cigarette as he walked and blew out a thick cloud of smoke. He'd just managed to give up cigarettes the week before. He was getting hooked again, and it was Eugene's fault. For two cents, he'd quit and go back and raise horses on the reservation. But that would bore him to death eventually. No, he'd just have to find some way to survive Jennifer. One day, he promised himself, he was going to walk out the door and leave Eugene with it.

Two

Jennifer Marist shared an office with several other geologists, a roomful of high-tech equipment, maps and charts and assorted furniture. On good days, she and the other geologists who worked for the Ritter Oil Corporation could maneuver around one another as they proceeded with their individual and collective projects. Unfortunately this wasn't a good day. Chaos reigned, and when the big boss himself, Eugene Ritter, asked Jenny to come into his office, it was a relief.

She took her time going down the long hall enjoying the glass windows that gave such a beautiful view of Tulsa, Oklahoma, and the lush vegetation that accented the walkway. Jenny was twenty-seven, but she looked much younger. Her long blond hair was soft and wavy, her deep blue eyes full of life and quiet pleasure. She wore a white knit sweater with simply designed gray slacks, but she still looked like a cover girl. It was the curse of her life, she thought, that men saw the face and not the personality and intelligence beneath it. Fortunately the men in her group were used to her by now, and none of them made sexist remarks or gave wolf whistles when she came into a room. They were all married except Jack, anyway, and Jack was fifty-six; just a bit old for Jenny's taste.

All told, though, Jenny had given up on the idea of marriage. It would have been lovely, but despite the modern world she lived in, the only two men she'd ever come close to marrying refused to share her with her globe-trotting career. They wanted a nice little woman who'd stay at home and cook and clean and raise kids. Jenny wouldn't have minded so much with the right man, but she'd spent years training as a geologist. She was highly paid and tops in her field. It seemed wasteful to sacrifice that for a dirty apron. But, then, perhaps she'd just never met the man she'd want to compromise for.

She glanced around as she entered the waiting room of Eugene's plush carpeted office, looking for Hunter. Thank God he was nowhere close by. She let out a tense sigh. Ridiculous to let a man get to her that way, especially a cold-blooded statue like Mr. Hunter. He was the company's troubleshooter and there had been a little trouble just lately. He and Jenny had partnered up for an evening to catch enemy agents who were after Jenny's top-secret maps of a potential new strike in strategic metals. It had been an evening to remember, and Jenny was doing her best to forget it all. Especially the part that contained him. They'd caught two men, but not the ringleader himself. Hunter had blamed her. He usually did, for anything that went wrong. Maybe he hated blondes.

She lifted her eyebrows at Betty, Eugene's secretary, who grinned and nodded.

"Go right in. He's waiting," she told Jenny.

"Is Hunter in there?" she asked, hesitating.

"Not yet."

That sounded ominous. Jenny tapped at the door and opened it, peeking around to find Eugene precariously balanced in his swivel chair, looking thoughtful.

"Come in, come in. Have a chair. Close the door first." He smiled. "How's the world treating you?"

"Fair to middling," she replied, laughing as she sat down in the chair across the desk.

He leaned forward, his silver hair gleaming in the light from the window behind him, his pale blue eyes curious. "Getting lonely since Danetta married my son and moved out?"

"I do miss my cousin," Jenny replied, smiling. "She was a great roommate." She leaned forward. "But I don't miss the lounge lizard!"

He chuckled. "I guess she misses him. Danetta's iguana is living with us, now, and my youngest son Nicky and he are best friends already. Cabe has promised Danetta a nice stuffed one for a pet anytime she wants it."

Jenny smothered a grin. Her employer's older son Cabe was well-known for his aversion to anything with scales; especially iguanas named Norman. Jenny had gotten used to the big lizard, after a fashion, but it was a lot more comfortable living without him.

"I've got a proposition for you," Ritter said without further preamble. "There's a piece of land down in Arizona that I want you to run a field survey on. I'll send down your equipment and you can camp out for a few days until you can get me a preliminary map of the area and study the outcroppings."

She knew she was going white. "The Arizona desert?"

"That's right. Quiet place. Pretty country. Peace."

"Rattlesnakes! Men with guns in four-wheel drives! Indians!"

"Shhhhh! Hunter might hear you!" he said, putting his finger to his lips.

She glared at him. "I am not afraid of tall Apaches named Hunter. I meant the other ones, the ones who don't work for us."

"Listen, honey, the Apaches don't raid the settlements anymore, and it's been years since anybody was shot with an arrow."

She glared harder. "Send Hunter."

"Oh, I'm going to," he said. "I'm glad you agree that he's the man for the job. The two of you can keep each other company. He'll be your protection while you sound out this find for me."

"Me? Alone in the desert with Hunter for several days and nights?" She almost choked. "You can't do it! We'll kill each other!"

"Not right away," he said. "Besides, you're the best geologist I have and we can't afford to take chances, not with the goings-on of the past month. And our adversary is still loose somewhere. That's why I want you to camp in a different section each night, to throw him off the track. You'll go to the target area on the second night. I'll show you on the map where it is. You aren't to tell anyone."

"Not even Hunter?" she asked.

"You can try not to, but Hunter knows everything."

"He thinks he does," she agrees. "I'll bet he invented bread..."

"Cut it out. This is an assignment, you're an employee, I'm the boss. Quit or pack."

She threw up her hands. "What a choice. You pay me a duke's ransom for what I do already and then you threaten me with poverty. That's no choice."

He grinned at her. "Good. Hunter doesn't bite."

"Want to see the teeth marks?" she countered. "He snapped my head off the night we lost that other agent. He said it was my fault!"

"How could it have been?"

"I don't know, but that's what he said. Does it have to be Hunter? Why can't you send that nice Mallory boy with me? I like him."

"That's why I won't send him. Hunter isn't nice, but he'll keep you alive and protect my investment. There isn't a better man for this kind of work."

She had to agree, but she didn't like having to. "Can I have combat pay?"

"Listen or get out."

"Yes, sir." She sat with resignation written all over her. "What are we looking for? Oil? Molybdenum? Uranium?"

"Best place to look for oil right now is western Wyoming," he reminded her. "Best place to look for moly is Colorado or southern Arizona. And that's why I'm sending you to Arizona—molybdenum. And maybe gold."

She whistled softly. "What an expedition."

"Now you know why I want secrecy," he agreed. "Hunter and you will make a good team. You're both clams. No possibility of security leaks. Get your gear together and be ready to leave at six in the morning. I'll have Hunter pick you up at your apartment."

"I could get to the airport by myself," she volunteered quickly.

"Scared of him?" Ritter taunted, his pale eyes twinkling at her discomfort.

She lifted her chin and glared at him. "No. Of course not."

"Good. He'll look after you. Have fun."

Fun, she thought as she left the room, wasn't exactly her definition of several days in the desert with Hunter. In fact, she couldn't think of anything she was dreading more.

Back in the office she shared with her colleagues, two of her co-workers were waiting. "What is it?" they chorused. "Moly? Uranium? A new oil strike?"

"Well, we haven't found another Spindletop," she said with a grin, "so don't worry about losing out on all that fame. Maybe he just thinks I need a vacation." She blew on her fingernails and buffed them on her knit blouse. "After all," she said with a mock haughty glance at the two men, "he knows I do all the work around here."

One of her co-workers threw a rolled-up map at her and she retreated to her own drafting board, saved from having to give them a direct answer. They all knew the score, though, and wouldn't have pressed her. A lot of their work was confidential.

She'd just finished her meager lunch and was on her way back into the building when she encountered a cold, angry Hunter in the hallway that led to her own office.

The sight of him was enough to give her goose bumps. Hunter was over six feet tall, every inch of him pure muscle and power. He moved with singular grace and elegance, and it wasn't just his magnificent physique that drew women's eyes to him. He had an arrogance of carriage that was peculiarly his, a way of looking at people that made them feel smaller and less significant. Master of all he surveys, Jenny thought insignificantly, watching his black eyes cut toward her under his heavy dark eyebrows. His eyes were deep-set in that lean, dark face with its high cheekbones and straight nose and thin, cruel-looking mouth. It wouldn't be at all difficult to picture Hunter in full Apache war regalia, complete with long feathered bonnet. She got chills just thinking about having to face him over a gun, and thanked God that this was the twentieth century and they'd made peace with the Apache. Well, with most of them. This one looked and sometimes acted as if he'd never signed any peace treaties.

In her early days with the company, she'd made the unforgivable mistake of raising her hand and saying "how." She got nervous now just remembering the faux pas, remembering the feverish embarrassment she'd felt, the shame, at how he'd fended off the insult. She'd learned the hard way that it wasn't politic to ridicule him.

"Mr. Hunter," she said politely, inclining her head as she started past him.

He took a step sideways and blocked her path. "Was it Eugene's idea, or yours?"

"If you mean the desert survival mission, I can assure you that I don't find the prospect all that thrilling." She didn't back down an inch, but those cold dark eyes were making her feel giddy inside. "If I got to choose my own companion, I'd really prefer Norman the Iguana. He's better tempered than you are, he doesn't swear, and he's never insulted me."

Hunter didn't smile. That wasn't unusual; Jenny had never seen him smile. Maybe he couldn't, she thought, watching him. Maybe his face was covered in hard plastic and it would crack if he tried to raise the corners of his mouth. That set her off and she had to stifle a giggle.

"Something amuses you?" he asked.

The tone was enough, without the look that accompanied it. "Nothing at all, Mr. Hunter," she assured him. "I have to get back to work. If you don't mind...?"

"I mind having to set aside projects to play guardian angel to a misplaced cover girl," he said.

Her dark blue eyes gleamed with sudden anger. "I could give you back that insult in spades if I wanted to," she said coldly. "I have a master's degree in geology. My looks have nothing whatsoever to do with my intelligence or my professional capabilities."

He lifted a careless eyebrow. "Interesting that you chose a profession that caters to men."

There was no arguing with such a closed mind. "I won't defend myself to you. This assignment wasn't my doing, or my choice. If you can talk Eugene into sending someone else, go to it."

"He says you're the best he has."

"I'm flattered, but that isn't quite so. He can't turn anyone else loose right now."

"Too bad."

She pulled herself up to her full height. It still wasn't enough to bring the top of her head any higher than Hunter's square chin. "Thank you for your vote of confidence. What a pity you don't know quartz from diamond, or you could do the whole job yourself!"

He let his gaze slide down her body and back up again, but if he found any pleasure in looking at her, it didn't show in those rigid features. "I'll pick you up at six in the morning at your apartment. Don't keep me waiting, cover girl."

He moved and was gone before she recovered enough to tell him what she thought of him. She walked back to her own office with blazing eyes and a red face, thinking up dozens of snappy replies that never came to mind when she actually needed them.

She pulled her maps of southern Arizona and looked at the area Eugene had pinpointed for her field survey. The terrain was very familiar; mountains and desert. She had topographical maps, but she was going to need something far more detailed before Eugene and his board of directors decided on a site. And her work was only the first step. After she finished her preliminary survey, the rest of the team would have to decide on one small area for further study. That would involve sending a team of geologic technicians in to do seismic studies and more detailed investigation, including air studies and maybe even expensive computer time for the satellite Landsat maps.

But right now what mattered was the fieldwork. This particular area of southern Arizona bordered government land on one side and the Apache reservation on the other. The reservation was like a sovereign nation, with its own government and laws, and she couldn't prospect there without permission. What Eugene hoped to find was in a narrow strip between the two claimed territories. He had a good batting average, too. Old-timers said that Eugene could smell oil and gold, not to mention moly.

It was too short a day. She collected all her equipment to be taken to the airport and the charts and maps she expected to have to refer to. With that chore out of the way, she went home.

Jenny cooked herself a small piece of steak and ate it with a salad, brooding over her confrontation with Hunter and dreading the trip ahead. He didn't like her, that much was apparent. But it shouldn't have affected their working relationship as much as it did. There were other women in the organization, and he seemed to get along well enough with them.

"Maybe it's my perfume," she murmured out loud and laughed at the idea of it.

No, it had to be something in her personality that set him off, because he'd disliked her on sight the first time they met.

She remembered that day all too well. It had been her first day on the job with the Ritter Oil Corporation. With her geology degree under her belt—a master's degree—she'd landed a plum of a job with one of the country's biggest oil companies. That achievement had given her confidence.

She'd looked successful that day, in a white linen suit and powder-blue blouse, with her blond hair in a neat chignon, her long, elegant legs in sheer hose, her face with just the right amount of makeup. Her appearance had shocked and delighted her male colleagues on the exploration team. But her first sight of Hunter had shocked and delighted *her*, to her utter dismay.

Eugene Ritter had called Hunter into his office to meet Jenny. She hadn't known about his Apache heritage then; she hadn't known anything about him except his last name. He'd come through the door and Jenny, who was usually unperturbed by men, had melted inside like warm honey.

Hunter had been even less approachable in those days. His hair had been longer, and he'd worn it in a short pigtail at his nape. His suit had been a pale one that summery day, emphasizing his darkness. But it was his face that Jenny had stared at so helplessly. It was a dark face, very strong, with high cheekbones and jet-black hair and deep-set black eyes, a straight nose and a thin, cruel-looking mouth that hadn't smiled when they were introduced. In fact, his eyes had narrowed with sudden hostility. She could remember the searing cold of that gaze even

now, and the contempt as it had traveled over her with
authority and disdain. As if she were a harem girl on dis-
play, she thought angrily, not a scientist with a keen analytical mind and meticulous accuracy in her work. It
occurred to her then that a geologist would be a perfect
match for the stony Mr. Hunter. She'd said as much to
Eugene and it had gotten back to Hunter. That comment
plus the other unfortunate stunt had not endeared her to
Hunter. He hadn't found it the least bit amusing. He'd
said that she wouldn't appeal to him if she came sliced and
buttered.

She sighed, pushing her last piece of steak around on
her plate. Amazing that he could hate her when she found
him so unbearably attractive. The trick fate had played on
her, she thought wistfully. All her life, the men who
wanted her had been mama's boys or dependent men who
needed nurturing. All she'd wanted was a man who was
strong enough to let her be herself, brains and all. Now
she'd finally found one who was strong, but neither her
brains nor her beauty interested him in the least.

She'd never had the courage to ask Hunter why he
hated her so much. They'd only been alone together once
in all the years they'd know each other, and that had been
the night they'd staged a charade for the benefit of the
agents who were after Jenny's survey maps.

They'd gone to a restaurant with Cabe Ritter and his
then-secretary, Danetta Marist, Jenny's cousin. Jenny had
deliberately worn a red, sexy dress to "live down to Hunter's opinion" of her. He'd barely spared her a glance, so
she could have saved herself the trouble. Once they'd
reached the apartment and the trap had been sprung,
she'd seen Hunter in action for the first time. The speed
with which he'd tackled the man prowling in her apartment was fascinating, like the ease with which he'd

floored the heavier man and rendered him unconscious.
He'd gone after a second man, but that one had knocked
Jenny into the wall in his haste to escape. Hunter had actually stopped to see that she was all right. He'd tugged
her gently to her feet, his eyes blazing as he checked her
over and demanded assurance that she hadn't been hurt.
Then he'd gone after that second man, with blood in his
eye, but he'd lost his quarry by then. His security men had
captured a third member of the gang outside. Hunter had
blamed Jenny for the loss of the second, who was the
ringleader. Odd how angry he'd been, she thought in ret-
rospect. Maybe it was losing his quarry, something he
rarely did.

She washed her few dishes before she had a quick
shower and got into her gown. The sooner she slept, the
sooner she'd be on her way to putting this forced trip behind her, she told herself.

She looked at herself in the mirror before she climbed
wearily into bed. There were new lines in her face. She was
twenty-seven. Her age was beginning to bother her, too.
Many more years and her beauty would fade. Then she'd
have nothing except her intellect to attract a husband, and
that was a laugh. Most of the men she'd met would trade
a brainy woman any day for a beautiful one, despite
modern attitudes. Hunter probably liked the kind of
woman who'd walk three steps behind her husband and
chew rawhide to make them soft for his moccasins.

She tried to picture Hunter with a woman in his arms,
and she blushed at the pictures that came to mind. He had
the most magnificent physique she'd ever seen, all lean
muscle and perfection. Thinking of him without the civ-
ilizing influence of clothes made her knees buckle.

With an angry sigh, she put out the light and got under
the sheets. She had to stop tormenting herself with these

thoughts. It was just that he stirred her as no other man ever had. He could make her weak-kneed and giddy just by walking into a room. The sight of him fed her heart. She looked at him and wanted him, in ways that were far removed from the purely physical. She remembered hearing once that he'd been hurt on the job, and her heart had stopped beating until she could get confirmation that he was alive and going to be all right. She looked for him, consciously and unconsciously, everywhere she went. It was getting to be almost a mania with her, and there was apparently no cure. Stupid, to be so hopelessly in love with a man who didn't even know she existed. At her age, and with her intellect, surely she should have known better. But all the same, her world began and ended with Hunter.

Eventually she slept, but it was very late when she drifted off, and she slept so soundly that she didn't even hear the alarm clock the next morning. But she heard the loud knocking on the door, and stumbled out of bed too drowsy to even reach for her robe. Fortunately her gown was floor-length and cotton, thick enough to be decent to answer a door in, at least.

Hunter glowered at her when she opened the door. "The plane leaves in two hours. We have to be at the airport in one. Didn't I remind you that I'd be here at six?"

"Yes," she said on a sigh. She stared up at his dark face. "Don't you ever smile?" she asked softly.

He lifted a heavy, dark eyebrow. "When I can find something worth smiling at," he returned with faint sarcasm.

That puts me in my place, she thought. She turned. "I have to have my coffee or I can't function."

"I'll make the coffee. Get dressed," he said tersely, dragging his eyes away from the soft curves that gown outlined so sweetly.

"But..." She turned and saw the sudden flash of his dark eyes, and stopped arguing.

"I said get dressed," he repeated in a tone that made threats, especially when it was accompanied by his slow, bold scrutiny of her body.

She ran for it. He'd never looked at her in exactly that way before, and it wasn't flattering. It was simply the look of a man who knew how to enjoy a woman. Lust, for lack of a better description. She darted into her room and closed the door.

She refused to allow herself to think about that smoldering look he'd given her. She dressed in jeans and a pink knit top for travel, dressing for comfort rather than style, and she wore sneakers. She left her hair long and Hunter could complain if he liked, she told herself.

By the time she got to the small kitchen, Hunter was pouring fresh coffee into two mugs. He produced cinnamon toast, deliciously browned, and pushed the platter toward her as she sat down with him at the table.

"I didn't expect breakfast," she said hesitantly.

"You need feeding up," he replied without expression. "You're too thin. Get that in you."

"Thank you." She nibbled on toast and sipped coffee, trying not to stare. It was heart-breakingly cozy, to be like this with him. She tried to keep her eyes from darting over him, but she couldn't help it. He looked very nice in dark slacks and a white shirt with a navy blazer and striped tie. He wore his hair short and conventionally cut these days, and he was the picture of a successful businessman. Except for his darkness and the shape of his eyes and the very real threat of his dark skills. He was an intimidating

man. Even now, it was hard going just to make routine
conversation. Jenny didn't even try. She just sat, working on her second piece of toast.

Hunter felt that nervousness in her. He knew she felt
intimidated by him, but it was a reaction he couldn't
change. He was afraid to let her get close to him in any
way. She was a complication he couldn't afford in his life.

"You talk more at work and around other people," he
remarked when he'd finished the piece of toast he'd been
eating and was working on his second cup of coffee.

"There's safety in numbers," she said without looking
up.

He looked at her until she lifted her head and then he
trapped her blue eyes with his black ones and refused to
let her look away. The fiery intensity of the shared look
made her body go taut with shocked pleasure, and her
breath felt as if it had been suspended forever.

"Safety for whom?" he asked quietly. "For you?" His
chin lifted, and he looked so arrogantly unapproachable
that she wanted to back away. "What are you afraid of,
Jennifer? Me?"

Yes, but she wasn't going to let him know it. She finished her coffee. "No," she said. "Of course not. I just
meant that it's hard to make conversation with you."

He leaned back in his chair, his lean, dark hand so large
that it completely circled the coffee mug. "Most people
talk a lot and say nothing," he replied.

She nodded. Her lips tugged up. "A friend of mine
once said that it was better to keep one's mouth closed and
appear stupid than to open it and remove all doubt."

He didn't smile, but his eyes did, for one brief instant.
He lifted the mug to his lips, watching Jenny over its rim.
She was lovely, he thought with reluctant delight in her
beauty. She seemed to glow in the early morning light,

radiant and warm. He didn't like the feelings she kindled in him. He'd never known love. He didn't want to. In his line of work, it was too much of a luxury.

"We'd better get going," he said.

"Yes." She got up and began to tidy the kitchen, putting detergent into the water as it filled the sink.

He stood, watching her collect the dishes and wash them. He leaned against the wall, his arms crossed over his chest. His dark eyes narrowed as they sketched the soft lines of her body with slow appreciation.

He remembered the revealing red dress she'd worn the night they'd staked out her apartment, and his expression hardened. He hoped she wasn't going to make a habit of wearing anything revealing while they were alone together. Jennifer was his one weak spot. But fortunately, she didn't know that and he wasn't planning to tell her.

"I'll get your suitcases," he said abruptly. He shouldered away from the wall and went out.

She relaxed. She'd felt that scrutiny and it had made her nervous. She wondered why he'd stared at her so intently. Probably he was thinking up ways to make her even more uncomfortable. He did dislike her intensely. For which she thanked God. His hostility would protect her from doing anything really stupid. Like throwing herself at him.

He had her bags by the front door when she was through. It was early fall, and chilly, so she put on a jacket on her way to the door. He opened the door for her, leaving her to lock up as he headed toward the elevator with the luggage. They didn't speak all the way to the car.

Three

——

Jenny was aware of Hunter's height as they walked to the car in the parking lot under her apartment building. He towered over her, and the way he moved was so smooth and elegant, he might have been gliding.

He put the luggage into the back of his sedan and opened the passenger door for her. He had excellent manners, she thought, and wondered if his mother had taught him the social graces or if he'd learned them in the service. So many questions she wanted to ask, but she knew he'd just ignore them, the way he ignored any questions he didn't want to answer.

He drove the way he did everything else, with confidence and poise. Near collisions, bottlenecks, slow traffic, nothing seemed to disturb him. He eased the car in and out of lanes with no trouble at all, and soon they were at the airport.

She noticed that he didn't request seats together. But the ticket agent apparently decided that they wanted them, to her secret delight, and put them in adjoining seats. That was when she realized how lovesick she was, hungry for just the accidental brush of his arm or leg. She had to get a grip on herself!

He sat completely at ease in his seat while she ground her teeth together and tried to remember all the statistics on how safe air travel really was.

"Now what's wrong?" he murmured, glancing darkly down at her as the flight attendants moved into place to demonstrate emergency procedures.

"Nothing," she said.

"Then why do you have a death-grip on the arms of your seat?" he asked politely.

"So that I won't get separated from it when we crash," she replied, closing her eyes tight.

He chuckled softly. "I never took you for a coward," he said. "Are you the same woman who helped me set up enemy agents only a few weeks ago?"

"That was different," she protested. She lifted her blue eyes to his dark ones and her gaze was trapped. Her breath sighed out, and she wondered which was really the more dangerous, the plane or Hunter.

He couldn't seem to drag his eyes from hers, and he found that irritating. At close quarters, she was beautiful. Dynamite. All soft curves and a sexy voice and a mouth that he wanted very much to kiss. But that way lay disaster. He couldn't afford to forget the danger of involvement. He had a life-style that he couldn't easily share with any woman, but most especially with a white woman. All the same, she smelled sweet and floral, and she looked so beautifully cool. He wanted to dishevel her.

He averted his face to watch the flight attendants go through the drill that preceded every flight, grateful for the interruption. He had to stop looking at Jennifer like that.

They were airborne before either of them spoke again.

"These people that you think are following us," she said softly, "is it the same group that broke into my apartment?"

"More than likely," he said. "You have to remember that strategic metals tend to fluctuate on the world market according to the old law of supply and demand. When a new use is found for a strategic metal, it becomes immediately more valuable."

"And an increase in one industry can cause it, too," she replied.

He nodded. She was quick. He liked her brain as much as her body, but he wasn't going to let her know that. "We didn't pick up the ringleader, you remember. He got away," he added with a cold glare at her.

She flushed. She didn't like being reminded of how helpless she'd felt. "I didn't ask you to stop to see about me," she defended.

He knew that. The memory of seeing her lying inert on the floor still haunted him. That was when he'd first realized he was vulnerable. Now he seemed to spend all his time trying to forget that night. The agents, his job to protect Jenny and the company, had all been momentarily forgotten when the agent knocked her down in his haste to get away. Hunter had been too shaken by Jennifer's prone position to run after the man. And that was what made him so angry. Not the fact that the agent had gotten away, but the fact that his concern for Jennifer had outweighed his dedication to his work. That was a first in his life.

"We're transferring to another flight in Phoenix, under different names," he said, lowering his voice. "With luck, the agents will pursue us on to California before they realize we're gone."

"How are we going to give them the slip? Are they on the plane?"

He smiled without looking at her. "Yes, they're about five rows behind us. We're going to get off supposedly to stretch our legs before the plane goes on to Tucson. We transfer to another airline, though, instead of coming back."

"What if they follow us?"

"I'd see them," he murmured dryly. "The rule of thumb in tracking someone is to never let your presence be discovered. Lose the subject first. This isn't the first time I've played cat and mouse with these people. I know them."

That said it all, she supposed, but she was glad she could leave all the details to him. Her job was field geology, not espionage. She glanced up at him, allowing herself a few precious seconds of adoration before she jerked her eyes back down and pretended to read a magazine.

She didn't fool Hunter. He'd felt that shy appraisal and it worried him more than the agents did. Being alone with Jennifer on the desert was asking for trouble. He was going to make sure that he was occupied tonight, and that they wouldn't set out until tomorrow. Maybe in that length of time, he could explain the situation to his body and keep it from doing something stupid.

It was a short trip, as flights went. They'd just finished breakfast when they were circling to land at the Tucson airport.

Hunter had everything arranged. Motel reservations, a rental car, the whole works. And it all worked to perfection until they got to the motel desk and the desk clerk handed them two keys, to rooms on different floors.

"No, that won't do," Hunter replied with a straight face, and without looking at Jennifer. "We're honeymooners," he said. "We want a double room.

"Oh! I'm sorry, sir. Congratulations," the clerk said with a pleasant smile.

Dreams came true, Jenny thought, picturing all sorts of delicious complications during that night together. The desk clerk handed him a key after he signed them in—as Mr. and Mrs. Camp. Nice of Hunter to tell her their married name, she thought with faint amusement. But it was typical of him to keep everything to himself.

He unlocked the door, waited for the bellboy to put their luggage and equipment in the room, and tipped the man.

They were alone. He closed the door and turned to her, his dark eyes assessing as he saw the faint unease on her face. "Don't start panicking," he said curtly. "I won't assault you. This is the best way to keep up the masquerade, that's all."

She colored. "I didn't say a word," she reminded him.

He wandered around the room with some strange electronic gadget in one hand and checked curtains and lamps. "No bugs," he said eventually. "But that doesn't mean much. I'm pretty sure we're being observed. Don't leave the room unless I'm with you, and don't mention anything about why we're here. Is that clear?"

"Why don't we just go out into the desert and camp?"

"We have to have camping gear," he explained with mocking patience. "It's too late to start buying it now. The morning's over. We'll start out later in the afternoon."

"All right." She put her suitcases on the side of the room that was nearest the bathroom, hesitating.

"Whichever bed you want is yours," he said without inflection. He was busy watching out the window. "I can sleep anywhere."

And probably had, she thought, remembering some of his assignments that she'd heard about. She put her attaché case with her maps on the bed, and her laptop computer on the side table, taking time to plug its adapter into the wall socket so that it could stay charged up. It only had a few hours' power between charges.

"Give me that case," he said suddenly. He took the case with the maps and opened it, hiding a newspaper he'd brought into the case and then putting it in a dresser drawer with one of his shirts over it. The maps he tucked into a pair of his jeans and left them in his suitcase.

Jenny lifted an amused eyebrow. He had a shrewd mind. She almost said so, but it might reveal too much about her feelings if she told him. She unpacked her suitcase instead and began to hang up her clothes. She left her underthings and her long cotton gown in the suitcase, too shy of Hunter to put them in a drawer in front of him.

The gown brought to mind a question that had only just occurred. Should she put it on tonight, or would it look like an invitation? And worse, did he sleep without clothes? Some men did. She'd watched him put his things away out of the corner of her eye, and she hadn't seen either a robe or anything that looked like pajamas. She groaned inwardly. Wouldn't that be a great question to ask a man like Hunter, and how would she put it? Isn't this a keen room, Mr. Hunter, and by the way, do you sleep stark naked, because if you do, is it all right if I spend the night in the bathtub?

She laughed under her breath. Wouldn't that take the starch out of his socks, she thought with humor. Imagine, a woman her age and with her looks being that ignorant about a man's body. Despite the women's magazines she'd seen from time to time, with their graphic studies of nude men, there was a big difference in a photograph and a real live man.

"Is something bothering you?" he asked suddenly.

The question startled her into blurting out the truth. "Do you wear pajamas?" she asked, and her face went scarlet.

"Why?" he replied with a straight face. "Do you need to borrow them, or were you thinking of buying me a pair if I say no?"

She averted her face. "Sorry. I'm not used to sharing a room with a man, that's all."

No way could he believe that she'd never spent a night with a man. More than likely she was nervous of him. "We're supposed to be honeymooners," he said with faint sarcasm. "It would look rather odd to spend the night in separate rooms."

"Of course." She just wanted to drop the whole subject. "Could we get lunch? I'm starving."

"I want to check with my people first," he told her. "I've got a couple of operatives down here doing some investigative work on another project. I won't be long."

She'd thought he meant to phone, but he went out of the room.

Jenny sprawled on her bed, cursing her impulsive tongue. Now he'd think she was a simpleminded prude as well as a pain in the neck. Great going, Jenny, she told herself. What a super way to get off on the right foot, asking your reluctant roommate about his night wear. Fortunately he hadn't pursued the subject.

He was back an hour later. She'd put on her reading glasses, the ones she used for close work because she was hopelessly farsighted, and was plugging away on her laptop computer, going over detailed graphic topo maps of the area, sprawled across the bed with her back against the headboard and the computer on her lap. Not the best way to use the thing, and against the manufacturer's specs, but it was much more comfortable than trying to use the motel's table and chairs.

"I didn't know you wore glasses," he remarked, watching her.

"You didn't?" she asked with mock astonishment. "Why, Mr. Hunter, I was sure you'd know more about me than I know myself—don't you have a file on all the staff in your office?"

"Don't be sarcastic. It doesn't suit you." He stretched out on the other bed, powerful muscles rippling in his lean body, and she had to fight not to stare. He was beautifully made from head to toe, an old maid's dream.

She punched in more codes and concentrated on her maps.

"What kind of mineral are you and Eugene looking for?" he asked curiously.

She pursed her lips and glanced at him with gleeful malice. "Make a guess," she invited.

She realized her mistake immediately and could have bitten her lip through. He sat up and threw his long legs off the bed, moving to her side with threatening grace. He took the laptop out of her hands and put it on the table before he got her by the wrists and pulled her up against his body. The proximity made her knees go weak. He smelled of spicy cologne and soap, and his breath had a coffee scent, as if he'd been meeting his operatives in a café. His grip was strong and exciting, and she loved the feel of his body so close to hers. Perhaps, subconsciously, this was what she'd expected when she antagonized him . . .

"Little girls throw rocks at boys they like," he said at her forehead. "Is that what you're doing, figuratively speaking? Because if it is," he added, and his grip on her wrists tightened even as his voice grew deeper, slower, "I'm not in the market for a torrid interlude on the job, cover girl."

She could have gone through the floor with shame. The worst of it was that she didn't even have a comeback. He saw right through her. With his advantage in age and experience, that wasn't really surprising. She knew, too, from gossip that he disliked white women. Probably they saw him as a unique experience more than a man. She didn't feel that way, but she couldn't admit it.

"I'm not trying to get your attention. I'm tired and when I'm tired, I get silly," she said too quickly, talking to his shirt as she stiffened with fear of giving herself away. Odd, the jerky way he was breathing, and the fabric was moving as if his heartbeat was very heavy. Her body was melting, this close to his. "You don't have to warn me off. I know better than to make a play for you."

The remark diverted him. "Do you? Why?" he asked curtly.

"They say you hate women," she replied. "Especially," she added, forcing her blue eyes up to his narrowed dark ones, "white women."

He nodded slowly. His gaze held hers, and then drifted down to her soft bow of a mouth with its faint peach lipstick, and further, to the firm thrust of her breasts almost but not quite touching his shirtfront. He remembered another beautiful blond, the one who'd deserted him when he'd been five years old. Her Apache child had been an embarrassment in her social circles. By then, of course, her activist phase was over, and she had her sights on one of her own people. Some years back, he'd been taken in by a socialite himself. An Apache escort had been unique, for a little while, until he'd mentioned a permanent commitment. And she'd laughed. My God, marry a man who lived on a reservation? The memories bit into him like teeth.

He released Jennifer abruptly with a roughness that wasn't quite in character.

"I'm sorry," she said when she saw the expression in his dark eyes. She winced, as if she could actually feel his pain. "I didn't mean to bring back bad memories for you."

His expression was frightening at that moment. "What do you know about me?" he asked, his voice cutting.

She managed a wan smile and moved away from him. "I don't know anything, Mr. Hunter. Nobody does. Your life is a locked door and there's no key. But you looked..." She turned and glanced back at him, and her hands lifted and fell helplessly. "I don't know. Wounded." She averted her eyes. "I'd better get this put away."

Her perception floored him. She was a puzzle he'd never solved, and despite his security files, he knew very little about her own private life. There were no men at the office, he knew. She was discreet, if nothing else. In fact, he thought, studying her absently with narrowed eyes as she put away her computer, he'd never heard of her dating a man in all the years she'd been with the company. He'd never seen her flirt with a man, and even those she worked with treated her as just one of the boys. That fact had never occurred to him before. She kept her distance from men as a rule. Even out in the field, where working conditions were much more relaxed, Jennifer went without makeup, in floppy shirts and loose jeans, and she kept to herself after working hours. He'd once seen her cut a man dead who was trying to make a play for her. Her eyes had gone an icy blue, her face rigid with distaste, and even though she hadn't said much, her would-be suitor got the message in flying colors. Hunter wouldn't admit, even to himself, how that action had damned her in his eyes. Seeing her put in the knife had made him more determined than ever not to risk his emotions with her. There were too many hard memories of his one smoldering passion for a white woman, and its humiliating result. And, even longer ago than that, his mother's contempt for him, her desertion.

He turned away from Jennifer, busying himself with the surveillance equipment one of his cases contained. He redistributed the equipment in the case and closed it.

"Why do we have to have all that?" she queried suddenly.

He nodded toward her computer and equipment. "Why do you have to have all that?" he countered.

"It's part of my working gear," she said simply.

"You've answered your own question." He checked his watch. "Let's get something to eat. Then we'll have a look at camping supplies."

"The joy of expense accounts," she murmured as she got her purse and put away her reading glasses. "I wonder if Eugene will mind letting me have a jungle hammock? I slept in one when I was a kid. We camped next to two streams, and they were like a lullaby in the darkness."

"You can have a jungle hammock if you think you can find a place to hang it."

"All we need is two trees. . . ."

He turned, his hands on his lean hips, his dark face enigmatic. "The desert is notorious for its lack of trees. Haven't you ever watched any Western movies?" he added, and came very close to a smile. "Remember the Indians chasing the soldiers in John Wayne movies, and the soldiers having to dive into dry washes or gulches for cover?"

She stared at him, fascinated. "Yes. I didn't think you'd watch that kind of movie..." She colored, embarrassed.

"Because the solders won?" he mused. "That's history. But the Apache fought them to a standstill several times. And Louis L'Amour did a story called *Hondo* that was made into a movie with John Wayne." He lifted an eyebrow. "It managed to show Apaches in a good light, for once."

"I read about Cochise when I was in school. And Mangas Coloradas and Victorio..."

"Different tribes of Apache," he said. "Cochise was Chiricahua. Mangas and Victorio were Mimbreños."

"Which...are you?" she asked, sounding and feeling breathless. He'd never spoken to her like this before.

"Chiricahua," he said. His eyes searched her face. "Is your ancestry Nordic?" he asked.

"It's German," she said softly. "On my father's side, it's English." Her eyes wandered helplessly over his lean face.

Her intense scrutiny disturbed him in a new and unexpected way. Her eyes were enormous. Dark blue, soft, like those of some kitten. He didn't like the way they made him tingle. He turned away, scowling.

"We'd better go, Jennifer."

Her name on his lips thrilled her. She felt alive as never before when she was with him, even if it was in the line of duty.

She started toward the door, but he turned as she reached it, and she bumped into him. The contact was like fire shooting through her.

"Sorry!" She moved quickly away. "I didn't mean to...!"

He put a strong hand under her chin and lifted her face to his eyes. Her eyelids flinched and there was real fear in them at close range. "You really are afraid of me," he said with dawning comprehension.

She hadn't wanted him to know that. Of course she was afraid of him, but not for the reasons he was thinking. She moved back and lowered her eyes. "A little, maybe," she said uneasily.

"My God!" He jerked open the door. "Out."

She went through it, avoiding him as she left. She hadn't expected the confession to make him angry. She sighed heavily. It was going to be a hard trip, all the way, if this was any indication. He was coldly silent all the way to the motel restaurant, only taking her arm when they were around people, for appearance's sake.

They were halfway through their meal when he spoke again.

"It's been years since I've scalped anyone," he said suddenly, his angry eyes searching hers.

The fork fell from her fingers with a terrible clatter. She picked it up quickly, looking around nervously to see if anyone had noticed, but there was only an old couple nearby and they were too busy talking to notice Jennifer and her companion.

She should have remembered how sensitive he was about his heritage. She'd inadvertently let him believe that she was afraid of him because he was an Indian. What a scream it would be if she confessed that she was afraid of him because she was in love with him. He'd probably kill himself laughing.

"No, it's not that," she began. She stopped, helplessly searching for the right words. "It's not because you're..." She toyed with her fork. "The thing is, I'm not very comfortable around you," she said finally. She put down her fork. "You've never made any secret of the fact that you dislike me. You're actively hostile the minute I come into a room. It isn't exactly fear. It's nerves, and it has nothing to do with your heritage."

She had a point. He couldn't deny that he'd been hostile. Her beauty did that to him; it made him vulnerable and that irritated him. He knew he was too touchy about his ancestry, but he'd had it rough trying to live in a white world.

"I don't find it easy, living among your people," he said. He'd never admitted that to anyone before.

"I can imagine," she replied. Her eyes searched his. "You might consider that being a female geologist in an oil company isn't the easiest thing to do, either. I loved rocks."

His dark eyes conquered hers suddenly. The look was pure electricity. Desert lightning. She felt it all the way to her toes.

"I find you hard going, too, Miss Marist," he said after a minute. "But I imagine we'll survive. Eugene said we were to camp on the actual site the second night."

"Yes." Her voice sounded breathless, choked.

He found himself studying her hand on the table. Involuntarily his brushed over the back of it. He told himself it was for appearances. But touching her gave him pleasure, and she jumped. He scowled, feeling her long fingers go cold and tremble. His eyes lifted back to hers. "You're trembling."

She jerked her hand from under his, almost unbalancing her water glass in the process. "I have to finish my steak." She laughed nervously. "The stores will close soon."

"So they will."

The subterfuge didn't fool him, she knew. Not one bit. His chin lifted and there was something new in the set of his head. An arrogance. A kind of satisfied pride that kindled in his eyes.

He was curious now. A beautiful woman like Jennifer would be used to giving men the jitters, not the reverse. He let his gaze fall to her soft mouth as it opened to admit a small piece of steak, and he felt his body go rigid. Over the years, he'd only allowed himself the occasional fantasy about making love to her. As time passed, and he grew older, the fantasies had grown stronger. He could keep the disturbing thoughts at bay most of the time. But there was always the lonely night when he'd toss and turn and his blood would grow hot as he imagined her mouth opening for him, her hands on his back, her soft legs tangling with his in the darkness. Those nights were hell. And the next few, alone with her, were going to sorely test his strength of will. For her it would be a field expedition. For him, a survival course, complete with sweet obstacles and pitfalls.

He had to remember that this was an assignment, and enemy agents were following them. Strategic metals always drew trouble, not only from domestic corporations struggling to get their hands in first, but from foreign investors interested in the same idea. He had to keep his mind on his work, and not on Jennifer. But her proximity wasn't going to make that job any easier. He almost groaned aloud at the difficulties. There hadn't been a woman in a long time, and he was hungry. He wanted Jennifer and he was relatively sure that she was attracted to him. She was certainly nervous enough when he came close.

But, he thought, what if her fear of him was genuine and had nothing to do with attraction? Her explanation that it was because they were enemies didn't hold up. It was far too flimsy to explain the way she trembled when he touched her hand. Fear could cause that, he had to admit. And he had been unkind to her, often. He sighed heavily. Thinking about it wasn't going to make it any easier.

They went to a hardware store when they finished their meal, and Jennifer watched him go about the business of buying camping supplies with pure awe. He knew exactly what to get, from the Coleman stove to the other gear like sleeping bags and tent and cans of Sterno for emergencies. Jennifer had gone out into the field before, many times, but usually there was some kind of accommodation. She hadn't relished the idea of camping out by herself, although she loved it with companions. Hunter, though, was going to be more peril than pleasure as a tentmate. She had to get a grip on herself, she told her stubborn heart again. The prospect of a few nights alone with him was sending her mad.

He loaded the gear into the four-wheel drive vehicle he'd had waiting for them at the airport. It was a black one, and he drove it with such ease that she suspected he had one of his own at home. That brought to mind an interesting question. Where was home to him? She knew he had an apartment in Tulsa, but he spent his time off in Arizona. Near here? With a woman, perhaps? Her blood ran cold.

"We'll be ready to go in the morning," he told her when they were back in the motel room again, with their gear stowed in the locked vehicle outside. All except her computer and his surveillance equipment, of course. He wasn't risking that. "Do you want to shower first?"

She shifted uncomfortably. "If you don't mind."

"Go ahead. I'll watch the news."

She carried her things into the bathroom, firmly locking the door, despite what he might think about the sound. She took a quick shower and put on clean blue jeans and a clean white knit shirt. She felt refreshed and sunny when she came back out, her face bright and clean without makeup.

He was sprawled across a chair, his shoes off, a can of beer in his hand. He lifted an eyebrow. "Do you mind beer, or does the smell bother you?"

"No. My father likes his lager," she said as she dealt with her dirty clothes.

He finished his drink and stood, stripping off his shirt. "If you're finished, I'll have my shower. Then we'll think about something for dinner."

She was watching him as helplessly as a teenage girl staring at a movie star. He was beautiful. God, he was beautiful, she thought with pleasure so deep it rivaled pain. Muscles rippled in his dark torso from the low-slung belt on his jeans to the width of his shoulders as he stretched, and her eyes sketched him with shy adoration.

He was aware of her scrutiny, but he pretended not to notice. He got a change of clothes to carry into the bathroom with him and turned, faintly amused by the way she busied herself with her computer and pretended to ignore him.

Her helpless stare had piqued his curiosity. He deliberately paused just in front of her, giving her an unnecessarily good view of his broad, naked chest.

"Don't forget to keep the door locked," he advised quietly, watching the flicker of her lashes as she lifted her blue eyes to his. "And don't answer it if someone knocks."

"Yes, sir, is that all, sir?" she asked brightly.

He caught her chin with a lean hand and his thumb brushed roughly over her mouth, a slow, fierce intimacy that he watched with almost scientific intensity. She knew her eyes were wildly dilated as they looked into his, and she couldn't help the shocked gasp that broke from her sensitized lips or the shiver of pleasure that ran through her body.

His dark eyes didn't miss a thing. Her reaction, he decided, was definitely not fear. He couldn't decide if he was pleased about it or not. "Don't be provocative," he said softly, his voice an octave deeper, faintly threatening. "Get to work." He moved away before she could find anything to say that wouldn't be provocative.

She sat down at her computer, her fingers trembling on the keyboard.

He closed the bathroom door behind him. His action had been totally unexpected, and it made her even more nervous than she already was. If he was going to start doing that kind of thing, she'd be safer in the lion cage at the zoo.

She was uncertain of him and of herself. Being around him in such close quarters was going to be a test of her self-control. She only hoped that she wouldn't give herself away. She'd had some naive idea that because Hunter disliked women, he didn't sleep with them. But she was learning that he knew a lot more than she did, and the

sultry look in his dark eyes really frightened her. If she
didn't watch her step, she was going to wind up with more
than she'd bargained for.

His motives were what bothered her most. He didn't
like white women, especially her, so what had prompted
that action? She didn't want to consider the most evident
possibility—that he thought she was fair game, and he
had seduction on his mind. She ground her teeth together. Well, he could hold his breath. She wasn't going
to be any man's light amusement. Not even his.

Four

When Jenny heard the shower running, she got up from her computer and sat in the chair Hunter had occupied to watch television. The chair still smelled of him. She traced the armrests where his hands had been and sighed brokenly. Jenny felt like a fool. She had to stop this!

She got out of the chair and went to work on her contour maps, trying to pinpoint the best place to look, given the mineral structure of the area. She'd begged time on Landsat earlier for another project, using the expensive computer time to study the satellite maps of this region of southern Arizona. The terrain they were going to survey was between the Apache reservation on one side and government land on the other. A narrow strip of desert and a narrow strip of mountain made up the search area, although they were going to be camping in several different spots to throw any would-be thieves off the mark.

She was deep in concentration when Hunter came back out of the bathroom, wearing clean jeans and no shirt, again. She had to bite her lip to keep from staring at him. He was unspeakably handsome to her, the most attractive man she'd ever known, but she couldn't afford the luxury of letting him know that. Especially not after the way he'd touched her mouth . . .

"Found what you're looking for?" he asked, placing one big hand on the table beside her and resting the other on the back of her chair. He leaned down to better see what she was studying. His cheek brushed hers and he felt her jump. His own breath caught. He wanted her. He should never have agreed to come on this expedition, because being close to her was having one hell of a bad effect on his willpower and self-control. He'd thought of nothing except the vulnerable look in her eyes when he'd touched her mouth so intimately, the yielding, the fascination. He wanted to grind his mouth into her own and make her cry out her need for him.

She was feeling the same tension. She knew he sensed her reaction, but she kept her head. "You startled me," she said breathlessly.

He knew better. His lean, warm cheek was touching hers as he stared at the map on the computer's small screen. She looked sideways and saw the thick, short lashes over his dark eyes, the faint lines in his cream-smooth tan. "Hunter . . ." His name was a soft whisper that broke involuntarily from her throat.

His head turned, and his eyes looked deeply into hers from scant inches away. She could taste his breath on her mouth, smell the clean scent of his body, feel the impact of his bare arms, his chest. He intoxicated her with his nearness, and she saw the hot glitter of awareness in those black eyes. She could see the thick dark lashes above them lower as his gaze suddenly dropped with fierce intent to her parted lips.

She shivered. All her dreams hadn't prepared her for the impact of this. Like a string suspended from a height, waiting for the wind to move it, she hung at his lips without breathing. A fraction of an inch, and his mouth would be on hers...!

The knock at the door startled them both. Hunter stared at her and cursed himself for his own vulnerability. She was intoxicating him, damn her. He was a new experience for her, that was all. He had to get himself under control.

He jerked erect and moved to the door. "Yes?" he asked as he opened it.

"Mr. Camp?" a feminine voice said loudly enough that anyone listening could hear. "I'm Teresa Whitley." A tall brunette moved into Jennifer's line of vision. The woman was smiling up at Hunter. "You requested some information about tour spots?"

"Inside," he said, holding the door open. He actually smiled at the woman, and Jennifer wanted to scream.

"Miss Marist?" Teresa smiled warmly, extending a hand as Jennifer came forward. They shook hands. "Nice to meet you. I'm with the corporation—under Mr. Hunter, in fact, so I'd better call you Mrs. Camp outside this room."

"Good idea," Jennifer replied absently. She was still vibrating.

"I've got some more information for you about the area. It's all here, on disk." She frowned. "I'm still learning about computers, I'm afraid. You do use the 3½ inch diskettes in your laptop?"

"I have a hard disk drive," Jennifer told her. "But I can use the diskettes as well."

"Thank goodness!" She handed the diskette, in its plastic case, to Jennifer. "I'm afraid I don't know much about science." She sighed, and her dark brown eyes sought Hunter's flirtatiously. "I'm just a security officer, so I deal with people instead of machines."

And, oh, I'll just bet you do it well, Jennifer thought. She didn't say so. She murmured something about checking out the new data and went back to her computer.

"If you'd like, we can run by the office and I'll give you the results of that security check you had us run," she told Hunter. "We could have dinner afterward, if you haven't already eaten?"

Jennifer ground her teeth together. She knew now what Hunter had meant earlier when referring to his "other project." This was it, and it had brown eyes and a svelte figure. Jennifer wished she'd dressed to the hilt and put on her makeup. In full regalia, she could have given that exotic orchid a run for her money, but she'd thought dressing up might give Hunter wrong ideas about her.

"Fine," Hunter replied tersely. "Let me get my shirt on."

Finally, Jennifer thought. He hadn't bothered before, but perhaps he didn't want to drive Miss Security Blip out of her mind by flashing his gorgeous muscles.

Hunter glanced at Jennifer, watching the way she studiously ignored Teresa, not to mention him. He glared at her as he pulled a pale gray knit shirt out of his drawer and put it on. He ran a comb through his hair, with Teresa sighing audibly over him.

"You haven't met Teresa before, I gather, Jennifer?" he asked too casually.

"No," she replied, forcing a smile.

"She's Papago." He said it with bitter pleasure, knowing Jennifer would catch the hidden meaning. This woman was Indian.

"Tohono O'Odham," Teresa teased. "We changed our name from 'bean people' in Zuni to 'people of the desert' in Papago."

"Sorry," he said with a smile.

Jennifer hated that damned smile. She'd never seen it, but this woman was getting the full treatment. Of course, Teresa wasn't a blond scientist, she thought darkly. Well, he needn't think she was going to play third fiddle while he courted his secret agent here.

"I'd rather you stayed here...." he began as Jenny said, "I have a headache...."

He cocked an eyebrow and she cleared her throat.

"I'll order something from room service," she continued. "If I feel like eating later," she amended without looking at him. "I've spent too much time at the laptop. The screen bothers my eyes." God knew why she was trying to justify her nonexistent headache. He and his brunette wouldn't notice.

"I hope you feel better," Teresa said.

"Thanks."

"Shall we go?" Hunter asked as he pulled on his tan sports coat over his knit shirt. He turned at the door. "Keep the door locked. If you have room service, check credentials before you let anyone in here."

"Yes, sir," she said with resignation.

He let Teresa out and started to close the door. He looked back at Jennifer first, and the intensity of his stare made her lift her head. His eyes held hers for one long moment before they went to her mouth and back up again.

"Don't wait up," he said, but there was another, darker meaning in the casual remark.

"You can depend on me, sir," she saluted him.

He shook his head and went out the door.

She picked up one of her shoes and threw it furiously at the closed door. It connected a split second before he opened it again. The expression on his face was priceless, she thought.

"I forgot my car keys," he said, watching her narrowly as he went to the dresser to get them. On the way back, he reached down and picked up her shoe, cocking an eyebrow at it. "Target practice?"

She tried to look innocent. "Would I throw a shoe at you?"

He studied her for a long moment before he dropped the shoe on the floor. "I'll be back before midnight. You should be safe enough."

"Definitely safer than Miss Whitley," she said, and could have bitten her tongue clean through.

His head lifted. "That's true. Most men react to a deliberate invitation. Even me," he added, angry at his vulnerability and lashing out because of it.

Her face colored. "I did not—" she began.

"Invite me?" He let his eyes drop slowly to her mouth. "Yes, you did. But it won't work a second time. You're not my type, cover girl," he added with a mocking smile. "I like a woman with less experience than I have. Not more."

He went out without a backward glance, missing the fierce anger that burned in her cheeks. She hadn't invited him! She groaned. Yes, she had. She wanted him and it showed, but he thought it was because she was experienced and used to a full sexual life. What a laugh!

She went back to her computer. Anyway, he'd just warned her off, and maybe it was a good thing. He seemed to prefer Miss Whitley, and he could relate to her. She was from his world, and Jennifer was just a diversion that shouldn't have happened.

She glanced at her reflection in the mirror and sighed angrily. "You should have stayed home in Missouri and married a mountain man and had two point five children," she told herself. "Instead of joining an oil company and getting tangled up with Mr. Native American."

She refused to let herself think about that one weak moment she'd shared with Hunter. She ordered a fish dinner and coffee to be sent to the room, and she ate it in silence, hoping the fish would leave its scent and drive him crazy. She'd heard someone say that he hated fish. Good enough for him. She hoped his girlfriend gave him warts.

It was only ten o'clock when she put on her cotton gown—deciding to let Hunter think what he liked— climbed into bed and turned out the lights. She didn't mean to go to sleep, she was too fired up by the long day and longer evening. But she was tired and the day caught up with her. She closed her eyes and slept like a baby.

Hunter came in just after midnight, sick of Miss Whitley's too-obvious adoration, and found Jennifer sprawled on her bed in a gown that would have raised a statue's temperature.

The covers had been thrown off, and the gown was up around her thighs. She was lying on her back with one arm thrown over her head, and the bodice was half off, baring the exquisite pink curve of one firm breast. Her clothes hid most of her figure. She didn't seem to go in for revealing things, except for that one night when she'd sent him up the walls in a low-cut red dress that showed every man around just what he was missing.

She was no less lovely now in that white cotton gown with its delicate embroidery. With her long blond hair spread around her perfect oval of a face, her lips parted in sleep, her body totally relaxed, she made a picture that he was going to have hell forgetting.

He managed to turn away from her at last and stripped down to his shorts. He almost removed them, too, but her remark about pajamas came back to twist his lips into a smile. He turned back his covers and set one of the security devices, just in case. From what Teresa had found out for him, the agent had been misled by this "vacation trip" and had followed their flight on to California, not realizing that Hunter and Miss Marist had suddenly turned into Mr. and Mrs. Camp in Tucson. But it didn't pay to get careless.

He had to remember that, he thought, looking at Jennifer one last time before he turned out the light. It had been one close call tonight, when Teresa had interrupted them. Another few seconds, and he'd have taken Jenny's sweet mouth without one single thought for the consequences. She'd have let him. That memory haunted him until he fell asleep. For a woman who purported to hate him, she was remarkably responsive to his touch. He had to convince her that he wasn't interested, no matter what it took. Her responsiveness could have terrible consequences if he let himself take advantage of it.

The next morning, Hunter was awake and dressed and had breakfast waiting when Jennifer smelled the coffee and food and forced her eyes open.

She sat up, barely aware of her state of undress until she saw Hunter scowl and avert his eyes. She tugged down her gown, angry at having given him a show, and quickly got her clothes together to dress in the bathroom.

She fixed her hair and put on makeup this morning, and she was wearing a blouse for a change, one that buttoned up and emphasized the exquisite shape of her breasts and her narrow waist. It was red, to go with her white jeans, and as she looked at her reflection, she hoped Hunter had fits because of her outfit. Miss Whitley, indeed! This morning she was more than match for the security lady.

When she went back into the room, Hunter was dishing up eggs and bacon. "Coffee's in the pot, pour your own," he said curtly.

"Thanks." She took the plate from him, aware of her beauty and its effect, tingling when she saw his dark eyes glance over her body and away.

"We aren't going to a party," he informed her curtly.

Her eyebrows arched. "Jeans, a short-sleeved blouse and sneakers aren't exactly party gear," she pointed out.

He lifted his head, and his eyes made threats. "I'm not a eunuch. We're going out into the desert, where we'll be completely on our own for several days. Don't complicate things. You looked better yesterday."

"Did I? Compared to what?" she demanded coldly. "Or should I say to whom?"

He let out a heavy sigh and leaned back in his chair to study her. "Teresa is an operative. When she isn't trying to compete for attention, she's very good at her job. I'm not her lover, nor likely to be. Nor yours," he added with a cold stare.

She had to grit her teeth. "I wasn't inviting you to be my lover. I'm tired of knit blouses. It gets hot on the desert. This blouse is cooler. So are the white slacks—they tend to reflect heat."

"God deliver me from scientific lectures before breakfast," he said icily, his narrow dark eyes making her ner-

vous. "The fact is, Miss Marist, you saw Teresa as
competition and you wanted to show me that you could
beat her hands down in a beauty contest. All right, you
have. You win. Now put on something less seductive and
eat your breakfast. I'd like to get started."

She shook with mingled fury and humiliation and in-
dignation, her fists clenched at her sides. No man had ever
enraged her so much, so easily. She could have laid a chair
across his skull with pleasure. Except that he was right.
She *had* been competing for his attention. She just hadn't
wanted him to realize it.

She grabbed up the same white knit shirt she'd worn the
day before and pulled it on over her blouse, tugging her
shirt collar through the rounded neckline. She didn't say
another word to him. She sat down at the table and ate her
breakfast. She was getting used to not tasting what she ate
when she was with him. One way or another, he always
managed to kill her appetite.

He finished his bacon and eggs and leaned back to sip
his coffee, his gaze level and speculative. "Pouting?" he
taunted. He wanted her and he couldn't have her. It was
making him irritable. "You should know better than to
throw yourself at men."

Her dark blue eyes flashed fire. She put down her coffee cup. "I don't pout," she said coldly, getting to her
feet. "And I don't need to throw myself at men! Especially you!"

He got up, too, towering over her, his eyes dark with
mingled frustration and anger. It got worse when she tried
to step back and her cheeks flushed.

"To hell with it," he murmured roughly. He caught her
waist and jerked her against his lean, powerful body,
holding her there while his mouth bent to hers.

He didn't look in the least loverlike. He looked furious. "Hunter, no . . . !" she whispered frantically, pushing at his chest.

His lips poised just above hers, his dark eyes holding hers, his breath on her face. "You're going to push until you find out, aren't you?" he asked roughly. "Well, for the book, Apaches don't kiss their women on the mouth. But I'm no novice with your race or your sex. So do let me satisfy your curiosity."

The tone was smooth and deep, pure honey. She watched his hard lips part and then they were on her mouth, fierce and rough but totally without feeling. His breath filled her mouth with its minty warmth, his mouth moved with expert demand. But his body showed no sign of arousal, and he might have been holding a statue for all the warmth he projected.

She'd wanted this. She'd waited forever to be close to him like this, to feel his arms closing around her, enfolding her, to feel his hard mouth on hers. She breathed him, anguished pleasure racking her body at the taste of him, so intimate on her mouth.

But he was feeling nothing, and she realized it quite suddenly, with bitter disappointment. Almost at once he lifted his head. She opened her eyes and saw nothing in his face. No desire, nor need, nor love. There was nothing there except a cold curiosity. She was hungry, but he wasn't. Not a hair out of place, she thought with faint hysteria, Mr. Cool.

He let her go with a smooth, abrupt movement of his hands, putting distance between them effortlessly. "If you know as much about men as I think you do," he said quietly, "that should tell you exactly what I feel." He smiled, but it was a mocking, cold smile. "Bells didn't ring. Horns didn't blow. The earth didn't move. You have a pretty mouth, but I wouldn't kill for it. So now that we've breached that hurdle, can we go to work?''

She swallowed her pride and hurt. "By all means," she said. "I'll get my gear."

It was dark and they were camped on the peak of a small hill, under a palo verde tree. No jungle hammock, just a tent with two sleeping bags inside it. The bags were positioned as far apart as Jennifer could get them. Equipment was set up to monitor any movement for miles around. The computer was busy. There was no conversation. Jenny hadn't said one single word to Hunter since they left the motel, and if she had her way, she never would again. She didn't care about him, she told herself. She couldn't love a man who could be that cruel.

He was aware of her hostility, but he preferred it to those melting glances she'd been giving him. He'd deliberately been ice-cold with her when he'd kissed her. It had been imperative to show her that he felt nothing. Now he'd convinced her, and he wasn't pleased with his handiwork.

Jenny had withdrawn from him, into her work. Now it was she who was ignoring him, and it disturbed him to feel the distance he'd created. Not that it wasn't desirable. He couldn't afford the luxury of involvement with Ritter's top field geologist. It would complicate his own job, especially when the affair ended. And it would end. He and Jennifer were as different as night and day. He wanted her. She wanted him. But desire would never be enough to keep them together. He was old enough to know that, and she should be.

She was so different like this. They'd never been alone together on assignment, there had always been other people around. He saw a Jennifer that he hadn't known existed. A shy, uncertain woman with a keen analytical mind who actually downplayed her extraordinary looks. Or she had, he amended, until Teresa had tried her hand at upstaging Jennifer. Jennifer had tried to compete, to draw his attention. He should be flattered, he supposed, but it had made him angry to be the object of a female tug-of-war.

"Do you want anything to eat?" he asked when the silence became too tense.

"I had a candy bar, thanks," she replied. She was putting away the computer, her attention elsewhere.

"I brought provisions. You can have anything you like, including a steak."

"I don't want anything."

"Starve yourself if you like," he said, turning his back to fix himself a steak on the Coleman stove. "Pride doesn't digest well."

"You'll never know," she said under her breath.

He glared at her. "Do you have to have every man you meet on your string?" he asked. "Does your ego demand blind adoration?"

She closed her eyes. The pain was unbearable. "Please stop," she said huskily. "I'm sorry. I won't do it again."

He felt a strange empathy with her at times. He seemed to sense her feelings, her emotions. He was doing it now. She was wounded, emotionally.

He got to his feet and knelt beside her, his dark eyes enigmatic. "Won't do what again?" he asked.

"I won't...how did you put it?...try to get your attention." She stared at the darkening ground. "I don't know why I tried."

He studied the shadows on the ground. Night was coming down around them. Crickets sounded in the grass.

A coyote howled. The wind caught her hair and blew it toward his face, and he felt its softness against his cheek.

"How old are you?" he asked suddenly.

"Twenty-seven," she replied, her voice terse because she didn't like admitting her age.

He hadn't realized she was that old. He frowned, wondering why on earth a woman so lovely should be so alone. "You don't date," he persisted.

"Checked the file, did you?" She pushed back her hair and glanced up at him and away as she closed the laptop and put it aside. "No, I don't date. What's the use? I was almost engaged twice, until they realized that I had a brain and wanted to use it. I wasn't content to be a room decoration and a hostess to the exclusion of my career. I've gotten used to being alone. I rather like it."

"Except sometimes on dark nights, when you go hungry for a man's arms," he added with faint insolence.

She stared at him with equal insolence. "I suppose you're in a position to know that," she agreed, nodding. "I've been alone too long, I suppose. Even you started to look good to me!"

He didn't answer her. He had to admit that he'd deserved that. He shouldn't have taunted her, especially about something that she probably couldn't even help.

She got up and moved away from him, tense and unnerved by his continued scrutiny.

"Come and eat something," he said.

She shook her head. "I meant it. I'm not hungry." She laughed bitterly. "I haven't tasted food since Eugene forced us on this ridiculous assignment. The only thing I want is to get it over with and get away from you!"

His dark eyes caught hers. "Do you, Jennifer?" he asked softly, his voice deep and almost gentle in the stillness.

She felt that tone to the soles of her feet and she turned away from him. It wasn't fair that he could do this to her. "I'd better get my equipment put away."

He watched her go. She seemed to bring out the very worst in him. "There's no need to run," he said mockingly, glaring at her through the growing darkness. "I'm not going to touch you again. I don't want you. Couldn't you tell?"

"Yes." She almost choked on the word. She turned toward the tent. "Yes, I could tell."

Her voice disturbed him. It seemed to hurt her that he didn't find her desirable. He drew in a slow breath, wondering what to do. It had seemed the best idea at the time, to put her at ease about his intentions. But he'd done something to her emotions with that cold, angry kiss. It hadn't been anything like the kiss he'd wanted to give her, either. Nothing like it.

He cooked his steak and ate it, feeling vaguely disturbed that he couldn't make her share it. He put out the fire, set his surveillance equipment, and went into the tent.

She was already in her sleeping bag, zipped up tight in her clothes, her eyes closed. But she wasn't asleep. He could hear her ragged breathing and there were bright streaks on her cheeks in the faint light of the flashlight he used to get to his own sleeping bag.

He put out the light angrily and took off his boots, climbing in fully clothed. He lay back on the ground, his eyes on the top of the tent, his mind full of thoughts, mostly unpleasant.

Jenny was crying. He could hear her. But to go to her, to offer comfort, would be the biggest mistake of all. He might offer more than comfort. Not wanting her was a lie. He did. He always had. But she'd want something more than desire, he thought. And desire was all he had to give.

She wiped at her tears, trying not to sniff audibly. She never cried, but she'd set new records tonight. Why did he have the power to hurt her so badly? She pushed the damp hair out of her eyes and stared at the wall of the tent, thinking back to camping trips with her parents and her cousin Danetta when they were girls. How uncomplicated and sweet life had been then. No career, no worries, just long lazy summer days and hope.

A coyote howled and she stiffened under the sleeping bag. Was it a coyote, or a wolf?

"It's a coyote," he said, giving it the Spanish pronunciation. "We call them songdogs. They loom large in our legends, in our history. We don't consider them as lowly as whites do."

"If you dislike white people so much, why do you work with us?" she asked angrily, her voice hoarse from the tears.

"It's a white world."

"Don't blame me. None of my ancestors ever served in the U.S. Cavalry out west. They were much too busy shooting Union soldiers."

"Was Missouri a southern state?"

"I'm not from Missouri originally. My parents moved there when I was seven. I was born in Alabama," she continued. "And that *is* a southern state."

"You don't have an accent."

"Neither do you."

He felt his lips tug into a smile. "Should I?"

"I wouldn't touch that with a pole, Mr. Hunter," she replied. "I've had enough of that big chip on your shoulder. I'm not aiming any more punches at it."

"Poles and chips and punches, at this hour of the night," he murmured gently.

"You don't have to talk to me, you know," she said wearily. "We can manage this assignment in sign language."

"Do you know any?" he asked in a dry tone as he crossed his arms over his head, stretching.

"A few phrases," she admitted, reluctant to confess it. "Eugene sent me up to Montana once and I had to parley with two Dakota Sioux. They spoke no English and I spoke no Sioux, so I learned to talk with my hands. It was very educational."

She was full of surprises. His head turned and he stared at her through the half darkness. "I could teach you to speak Apache."

She closed her eyes. "I don't want you to teach me anything, Mr. Hunter," she said huskily.

"Too bad," he replied, trying not to take offense. After all, he'd given her a hard time. "You could use a little tutoring. For an experienced women, you don't know much about kissing."

She couldn't believe what she was hearing. She sat up on the sleeping bag. "This from a man who already admitted that Apaches don't do it . . . !"

"That was back in the nineteenth century," he mused. He propped himself on one elbow and stared at her, his blood beginning to burn at the sight of her, so beautiful with her long hair around her shoulders. "How can you be twenty-seven and not know something so elementary as how to kiss a man properly?"

"You only did it to humiliate me . . . !"

"You didn't know that," he replied. He remembered her shy response, and it made him feel worse. Apparently the men in her life had been more interested in their own pleasure than hers, because no one had ever taught her about loveplay. He wanted to. His body went rigid as he realized how much he wanted to.

"I told you," she said, trying to salvage some of her pride. "I've been alone for a long time . . ."

"Have you? Why?" he asked.

She didn't want to go into why. He'd managed to cut her to the bone already with his cold manner, without the insult about the way she kissed. It hurt even more that he'd noticed, despite his lack of interest in her.

"Never mind," she said wearily. She lay back down and closed her eyes. "I just want to go to sleep. It's been a long day."

"So it has. We'll move camp tomorrow."

"Could we move it to Mars?" she asked. "It wouldn't make much difference, considering the lack of vegetation."

"You aren't seeing. The desert is alive and beautiful, if you know what to look for."

"You do, I suppose."

"I'm an Indian, remember?" he asked with rough insolence.

"How could I forget?" she muttered. "You never let anyone forget . . ."

"Go to sleep," he said shortly. He closed his own eyes, out of patience and totally out of humor. She was really getting to him. He turned his head on the sleeping bag and his eyes wandered slowly over the curve of her body under the quilted fabric. Damn Eugene, he thought furiously, closing his eyes against the sight of her. He'd never forgive him for this assignment.

Jennifer, meanwhile, was thinking much the same thing. He blew hot and cold, friendly one minute and hostile the next. She didn't know how to get along with him. He seemed to resent everything about her. Even the way she kissed, she thought bitterly. Well, hell would freeze over before she was going to kiss him again! She rolled over. Maybe in the morning, things would look better.

Five

But things didn't look better in the morning. Hunter was unapproachable. When he did glance her way, it was like an Arctic blast. Nothing she did was ever right, she thought ruefully.

She busied herself with getting her equipment together, trying not to let him know how hurt she was by his coldness. Worse, trying to forget the feel of him in intimacy, the hard expertness of his mouth on hers. Dreams had sustained her for so long. Now she had at least one bittersweet memory to tuck away. But like all memories and dreams, it wasn't enough.

They loaded the four-wheel drive and set off for the next site—the real one this time. It was back in a canyon, beside a stream under a nest of cottonwoods and oaks. Behind it was a mountain range, smooth boulders rising to jagged peaks high above and only a small rutted road through the dust to get to it.

"It's very deserted here," Jennifer murmured, thinking she wouldn't want to be here on her own. It was probably haunted....

"One of the old Apache camps," he said, looking around. "I feel at home." He glanced at her with faint menace. "But I can imagine that you don't. White captives were probably brought here."

She turned away. "If you don't mind sparing me your noble red man impersonation, I'd like to get my equipment."

He lifted an eyebrow. That was more like it. He'd grown weary of her attempts not to mention his ancestry or her embarrassment when she did.

"Apaches weren't the only tribe around here," he remarked as he lowered the tailgate and began removing equipment and sleeping gear. "Comanches roamed this far south, and Yaquis came up on raids from Mexico. There were bandidos, cavalry, cowboys and miners, gunfighters and lawmen who probably camped in this area." He glanced at her with a faint smile. "I hope that makes you less nervous."

Her eyebrows arched. "I'm not nervous... Oh!" She jumped when a yelp sounded somewhere nearby, and got behind Hunter, sheltering behind his broad shoulders.

He chuckled with pure delight, savoring that one surge of femininity from Miss Independence. "A coyote," he whispered. He glanced down at her as the yelps increased. "Fighting. Or mating," he added, his eyes burning into hers from scant inches.

She went scarlet, swallowed, and abruptly tore away from him with her heart beating her to death. It wasn't what he'd said, it was the way he'd said it, his black eyes full of knowledge, his voice like that of a lover.

"Could you set up the tent, so that I can get the portable generator hooked up to my laptop?" she said with shivering dignity.

He put down the sleeping bags and glanced at her. "What's wrong?"

"You're very blunt," she said stubbornly. "I wish you wouldn't go out of your way to make me uncomfortable."

His expression gave nothing away. He studied her curiously. "Did I embarrass you? Why? Mating is as natural as the rocks and trees around us. In fact," he added, his voice deepening, "some native tribes weren't that fanatical about purity in their young women. Adultery was the sin, not lovemaking."

She glanced at him angrily. "The Cheyenne were fanatical about maidenly purity, for your information," she told him curtly. "And the Apache were just as concerned with virtue..."

"Well, well," he murmured. "So you do read about Indian history?" A faint smile appeared on his dark face. "Do you find the subject interesting?"

Not for anything was she going to admit that she did because of him. She'd read extensively about the Apache, in fact, but she wasn't going to admit that, either.

Nevertheless, he suspected it. He pursed his lips. "Did you know that Apaches disliked children?"

"They did not," she said without thinking. "They even kept captive children when they raided, raising them as their own flesh and blood... Oops."

He laughed. His face changed, became even more handsome with the softness in his black eyes, the less austere lines of his face. "So they did," he murmured.

She turned away. "That wasn't kind."

"Why does it bother you to be curious?" he asked pleasantly. "I don't mind. Ask. I'll tell you anything you want to know about my people."

She put down her computer and her blue eyes searched his black ones. "I didn't want to offend you," she said. "You've always been reticent about your ancestry, especially with me. I know I got off on the wrong foot with you, right at the beginning," she added before he could speak. "You frightened me, and what I did, I did out of nervousness. I never meant to offend you."

"That was a wholesale apology," he murmured, watching her. "I'll add one of my own. You frightened me, too."

"Me?" She was astonished. "Why?"

His eyes darkened and he started to speak, but the sudden beat of helicopter blades diverted him. He looked up, glad that he'd parked the vehicle under the thick cover of the cottonwood trees.

He caught Jennifer's arm and propelled her close to the Jeep, at the same time reaching behind him, into his belt, for the .45 automatic he always carried.

The sight of the cold metal in his hand made her nauseous. Sometimes it was easy to forget exactly what he did for a living. But this brought it home with stark clarity. He knew how to use the gun, and probably had, many times. She knew he'd been shot a time or two, and she'd seen one of the scars against his tanned shoulder, when he'd taken a shower two nights earlier. She shivered, remembering how he earned his living, what risks he took doing it.

He felt her tremble and glared toward the departing sound of the helicopter. He'd never known her to be afraid. This had to be a first.

"It's all right," he said, feeling unusually protective toward her. "I won't let anyone hurt you."

She looked up at him, glad he'd misjudged the reason for her unsteadiness. "Thanks," she said huskily. She looked toward the canopy of leaves. "Was that them, do you think?"

"Very likely." He put the safety back on the automatic and reholstered it with practiced ease. "We'll make a smokeless fire, just in case."

She smiled at him. "I suppose woodcraft, or the desert equivalent, was part of your upbringing?"

He nodded. "One of my ancestors fought with Cochise," he said. "When I was a boy, I knew how to find water, which plants I could live on, how to find my way in the darkness. Did you know that an Apache can go without water for two days by sucking on pebbles?"

"Yes," she said simply. Her eyes lingered on his dark face. "I . . . read a lot," she explained.

He let his gaze fall to her soft mouth. He had to stop remembering how silky and warm it felt, like a rose petal kissed by the sun. She wasn't a woman he could have, ever. Not as long as they both worked for the corporation. It would be the kiss of death to become involved on the job. One of them would have to go, and that wouldn't be fair. Jennifer was good at her job, and she loved it. He loved his, as well. Better to avoid complications.

She frowned slightly. "What are you thinking?" she asked.

He smiled faintly. "That a hundred years or so ago, I could have carried you off on my pony and kept you in my wickiup," he murmured. "My other wives might have beaten or stoned you when I was out making war, of course."

"Other wives, the devil," she said firmly. "Polygamy or no polygamy, if I'd lived with you, there would have been one wife, and it would have been me."

He smiled at her ferocity. Amazing that she could look so cool and professional, but under the surface there was fire and independence and passion in her. He could imagine her with a rifle, holding off attackers and defending her home. Children playing around her skirts on lazy summer days. He frowned. His eyes fell to her flat stomach and for one insane moment, he let himself imagine...

"Why are you looking at me like that?" she asked softly.

His gaze came back up to hers, the expression in his eyes unreadable. "We'd better get things set up. I'll pitch the tent."

He became unapproachable again, withdrawing deep into himself. Jennifer was sorry, because just for a few minutes it had seemed that they were on the verge of becoming friendlier. But Hunter was Hunter again when he had the tent up and the portable battery backup working. He left her to her computer and charts, busying himself with securing the parameters of their small camp and setting up his distance surveillance equipment.

She put on a pair of hiking shorts and long socks with her thick-soled walking boots and a button-up khaki blouse. She had a hat, an Indiana Jones one, in fact, that she used to keep the sun from baking her head. One thing she'd learned long ago was that a hat in the desert was no luxury. One case of sunstroke had taught her that, and Hunter had given her hell when he'd found her lying on the ground far away in the Middle East, where they were working on assignment one time, searching for oil.

He glanced up when she came out in her working gear, nodding at the hat. "You remembered, I see," he remarked.

"You gave me hell," she recalled, smiling.

"You deserved it."

"Yes, I did. All the same, you got me to a medic in short order. You probably saved my life."

"I don't want hero-worship from you," he said flatly, staring back at her. "We'd better get going. Keep to the trees if you can. We know we're not alone. It's best not to take chances."

"The stream bed is where I want to be," she said coldly. "And it isn't hero-worship."

"No?" He gave her a mocking appraisal. "Then what is it?"

"Fascination," she said with a mocking smile of her own. "You're different."

He didn't betray so much as a flicker of an eyelash, but the words hit home. She'd accidentally betrayed what he'd suspected all along, that she coveted him because he was a new experience for her. Like another white woman, years before, who'd been entranced not by who he was so much as what he was.

"Different," she emphasized. "Hardheaded, cold-eyed, bad tempered, unpredictable and totally exasperating!"

None of which had anything to do with being Apache, he mused, relaxing a little. He smiled with reluctant amusement.

"I could go on," she added. "But I do have a job to do."

"I'm not the only one here with a bad temper," he replied as they started out. "And you have a hard head of your own."

"I wouldn't have a bad temper if you'd stop stripping around me," she blurted out.

His eyebrows arched. "When did I do that?"

"At the motel."

"Oh." He chuckled as he strode along beside her. "I wanted to see if it would affect you." He glanced down. "It did."

"Most men your age are as white as dead fish and flabby," she remarked, refusing to let him get to her. "I can't be the only woman who's ever found you fascinating without your shirt."

No, but she was the only one it mattered with, he admitted to himself. He found her equally disturbing, but it wasn't a good time to say so. His eyes were alert, watching for signs.

"Look!" she exclaimed, bending down at the creek where tracks were visible in the wet sand. "A cougar!"

He knelt down beside her. "So it is. How did you know?"

"Big print, no claw marks," she explained. "Dogs and wolves can't draw their claws back in like a cat can, and they leave claw marks. Look at this. It's a buck deer—cloven hoof print. A doe's is rounded."

He met her eyes with grudging admiration. "Tracking interests you, I gather?"

"It always has. My father hunts deer every fall. He taught me."

"Kill Bambi?" he exclaimed with mock horror.

It was the first real flash of amusement she'd seen in him. She laughed delightedly and impulsively pushed him. He fell heavily onto his side, laughing, too.

"You hellcat," he murmured, reaching out with a lightning movement to drag her down heavily against him. He rolled her in the damp sand, pinning her, his face hard, his eyes glittering with excitement as he loomed over her. His gaze went down to her breasts, where the buttons of her blouse had parted during the struggle, leaving her cleavage bare. His breath quickened as he looked at her, his expression changing from humor to intent male appreciation.

The feel of all that hard muscle so close made her tremble with pure need. She could smell the scent of his clothing, the cologne that clung to his skin. She looked up into his black eyes and knew in that moment that he was everything she'd ever want. She wanted him to bend down, to pin her body to the damp sand. She wanted his hard, warm mouth to crush into hers and kiss her senseless. She wanted him.

And the ferocity of her desire made her ache. "Kiss me," she whispered, unbearably hungry for him. She reached up and touched his lean, hard face with hands that trembled, loving the warm strength of him. "Hunter...!" She managed to lift herself enough to reach his hard mouth, and hers touched it with helpless need.

He froze at the contact, his breath catching as he felt her lips so soft and warm against his own. For one insane second he almost gave in to his own hunger. But she was off-limits. She had to be, because there was no future in it for either of them. He forced himself to go rigid, despite the fact that his damned heart was beating him to death as he struggled with desire.

His lean hands caught her wrists and he pushed her down, tearing her mouth from his as he loomed over her, looking cold and dangerous. "Stop it," he said curtly, forcing the words out.

She felt the rejection right through to her heart. He didn't want her, so why couldn't she stop offering herself? She hated having him know just how vulnerable she was. How could she have done something so stupid? She flushed beet red. Yes, she was vulnerable, but not Hunter. Mr. Native American was steel right through.

"Let me get up, please," she said, her voice trembling.

Pure bravado, and he knew it. He could have her, right here, and she'd give herself with total abandon. But he knew, too, that once would never be enough. He'd have her and then he'd die to have her again. The fever would never be satisfied.

He let go of her wrists and got to his feet, turning away to keep his vulnerability from her as he stared up at the mountains with apparent unconcern. God, that had been close! He wondered if he could ever forget the way he'd seen her, the sound of her soft voice begging for his kiss, the petal softness of her seeking lips on his mouth . . . !

Jenny shivered with reaction, barely able to breathe. She got up and her eyes went helplessly to his back. Well, he'd made his lack of interest clear enough. Maybe her body would eventually give up, she thought with hysterical humor. Despite her beauty, he simply did not want her. It was the most humiliating lesson of her life.

She looked away, gathering her savaged pride. "I'm supposed to be working," she said in a thready whisper.

"The sun's getting high," he said without looking at her. "Get your samples and then we'll find something to eat."

She felt totally drained. She picked up her hat with a shaken sigh and retrieved the backpack with her tools. She didn't even remember dropping it, she'd been so hungry for the touch of him.

His dark face gave nothing away as he glanced once at her and turned away. "Where do you want to look? And for what?" he asked curtly. "Gold? Is that why this operation is so secretive?"

She glanced up at him, twisting her contour map in her hands. "I know what you must be thinking," she said. She could still taste him on her mouth and it made her giddy. "Gold and Indians don't mix. White man's greed for it has cost the Native Americans most of their land."

"There was a flurry here a year or two ago when someone found a very small vein of gold," he said. "There were amateur prospectors everywhere, upsetting the habitat, invading private property, some of them even came on the reservation to dig without bothering to ask permission. The Bureau of Indian Affairs takes a very negative view of that kind of thing, and so does the tribal government."

"I don't doubt it. But gold isn't what I'm after right now. I'm looking for a quartz vein, actually."

"Quartz?" He glared at her. "Quartz is a worthless mineral."

"Perhaps, but it can lead to something that isn't. I'm looking for molybdenite ore."

He frowned. "What?"

"Molybdenum is a silver-white metallic chemical element, one of the more valuable alloying agents. It's used to strengthen steel, which makes it of strategic worth. Like oil, it's a rather boom-or-bust substance, because its value fluctuates according to demand. Back in 1982, weak market conditions led to the closure of most primary molybdenum mines. Now there's a new use for it, so it's back in demand again. The United States produces sixty-two percent of all the world's moly, and that's why we've got competition for new discoveries."

"So you're looking for molybdenum," he murmured, trying to follow the technical explanation.

"I'm looking for its source ore, molybdenite, a sulfide mineral. It looks very much like graphite, but its specific gravity and perfect cleavage differentiate it from that. It's found primarily in acid igneous rocks such as granite in contact metamorphic deposits, and in high-temperature

quartz veins. That's why I'm looking for quartz veins."
She smiled at his confusion. "Don't look so irritated, Mr.
Hunter. I couldn't fieldstrip an Uzi or set up surveillance
equipment, either. If what I'm doing is Greek to you,
what you do is another language to me, too."

That eased his bruised pride a little. He turned away.
"Then we'd better get going. This area looks promising,
you said?"

"Yes. The lay of the land and the mineral outcroppings I've found so far look very promising here."

"Moly. You say it's used to strengthen steel," he said,
watching her.

She nodded. "A very profitable mineral to mine, too.
There's already a deposit of it here in southern Arizona,
another one in Colorado."

"But if you found gold instead, you'd put a real feather
in your cap, wouldn't you?" he persisted, his eyes narrow and watchful.

"Oh, for heaven's sake!" She threw up her hands, her
blue eyes blazing with hurt and anger. "You just love to
think the worst of me, don't you? If I find gold, I'll take
out ads in all the national tabloids and give interviews and
send millions of people out here to harass the lo-
cals . . . !"

Involuntarily he put his thumb over her lips, stilling the
words. "All right," he said quietly. "My mistake," he
said, and his eyes fell to her mouth. His thumb moved
caressingly over it, and his body began to tense. Her lips
trembled under his touch. She was so vulnerable, and he
hated hurting her. He wanted her, too, but it was simply
impossible.

She couldn't bear to give herself away again. She drew
back from him, still wounded from his earlier harsh rejection. "I'll just take some samples here," she said in a

subdued tone, and without looking at him. "And get a few instrument readings."

He didn't say another word. But he was more watchful than ever for the rest of the day. He couldn't seem to take his eyes off her, and the more he looked, the more he wanted her. He almost groaned out loud when she stretched and he could see the sweet curves of her breasts outlined against the thin fabric of her blouse. She wouldn't deny him, and knowing it made the desire even greater. He had to get a grip on himself!

He prowled around his surveillance equipment, trying to get his mind off Jennifer's gorgeous body. When he couldn't prowl anymore, after dark, he stretched out on his sleeping bag and read by the light of the Coleman lantern while Jennifer rummaged in her suitcase.

Jenny was fascinated when she saw his books, the text indecipherable to her, despite her cursory knowledge of Spanish and French and a few words of Sioux.

"It loses something in the translation," he remarked when he noticed her interest. "I prefer the original language. This is Greek," he added, smiling faintly at her blush when she'd told him that what she was doing must seem like Greek to him.

She recovered quickly, though. "How did you learn Greek?"

"Overseas. I was CIA, didn't anyone tell you?"

She nodded, her eyes openly curious. "About that. And that you were in the special forces, and briefly a mercenary. You've done a lot of dangerous things, haven't you?"

"A few," he said, refusing to elaborate on it.

She gave up and busied herself getting a clean T-shirt and bra out of her suitcase. "It's dark. Do you think it would be all right if I bathed off a little of this dust? Are we safe here?''

"If you've got skinny-dipping in mind, I wouldn't advise it," he began.

"No, just my face and arms," she replied.

"Go to it. It's relatively protected here, and I've got sharp ears."

"Okay." She wanted some verbal reassurance that he wouldn't look, but he'd been withdrawn since they came back to camp. Probably she left him so cold that he wouldn't buy a ticket to see her totally nude. She felt terribly demoralized. Ironic, that men usually went crazy to have her, and Hunter wouldn't have her with cream and sugar.

The light from the smokeless camp fire gave her enough to see by. She pulled off her khaki blouse and, glancing behind at the half-closed tent flap, her bra. The cool water felt like heaven on her hot skin. She sponged herself off, thinking that Indian women must have bathed like this a century before, in this clean, cool glade with the sounds of crickets in the brush and the distant howl of coyotes or wolves and the faint swish of the trees when the wind blew.

Hunter tried to read his book, but the thought of Jennifer out there alone was too disturbing, especially after the chopper that had come so close. He didn't want to spy on her, but he justified his flash of conscience by telling himself that he'd been assigned to protect her.

He opened the tent flap and moved outside, silhouetted by the smokeless camp fire that was still burning under a pot of brewing coffee. Its dark, rich aroma filled his nostrils as he moved closer to the stream under the dark shadows of the trees.

Jennifer had her blouse and her bra off. He could see
her smooth, silky back in the firelight, see the white lines
where she'd sunbathed and the sun hadn't been able to
reach. Odd that she didn't sunbathe nude, with a body
like that, he thought stiffly.

He couldn't help looking. She half turned, her arms
uplifted as she dashed water on her breasts, and his breath
caught in his throat. They were full. Very full and very
firm, and tip-tilted. Her nipples were hard from the cold
water, dusky against the white streaks that cut across
where her bra would have been. His body tautened and he
felt himself beginning to tense with desire. He'd dreamed
of seeing her this way, but the reality was devastating.

Jennifer, unaware of his scrutiny, finished her half bath
and stretched, her body sensuously arched because the air
was just cool enough to be delicious on her bare skin, and
there was faint light from the nearly full moon. She
sighed, brushing her long blond hair away from her
freshly scrubbed face. The action lifted her breasts and
they were high and firm and softly glowing in the light
from the camp fire.

Hunter heard himself speaking, when he'd never meant
to betray his presence. "In the old days, the penalty for an
Apache warrior who spied on a woman at her bath was
death. The risk seems worth it to me right now, Jennifer.
I've never seen anything quite so beautiful."

His voice had startled her. She whirled from the big
rock she was sitting on, her body poised for flight, so
shocked by his eyes and nearness that she hadn't the
presence of mind to cover her breasts.

He was looking at them, too, with blatant appreciation, without even trying to hide that he was studying her.
"Your breasts are lovely," he said quietly, his voice a
whisper of deep tenderness in the night. "Much fuller

than I thought. Pink and mauve, like clouds on the horizon just at dawn when the sun touches them.''

Poetry, she thought dizzily. He was wooing her with words and she wanted his eyes so badly that she couldn't even do the decent thing and pretend to hide herself. All day she'd felt him watching her. If only he felt as she did, shared the fiery attraction that made her too weak to deny him now. She stood, proud in her seminudity, letting him look, feeding on his eyes. If that wasn't desire in his face now, she thought, awed, then she couldn't recognize it at all. He wanted her! The knowledge took away her reserve, her inhibitions. She walked toward him, her heart in her eyes.

His jaw tensed. He watched her come toward him and he ground his teeth together in one last effort at sanity. Her lips were parted, her eyes soft and hungry, her breasts rising and falling jerkily with her unsteady breathing.

She stopped just in front of him, her cheeks faintly ruddy with embarrassment and excitement. She couldn't have imagined doing this, but it seemed the most natural thing in the world. She looked up at him, meeting his dark, fierce gaze, trembling a little, because he looked capable of anything at that moment. For all her loving bravado, she was innocent and he wasn't. The complications of her actions could be extreme.

His chin lifted as he watched her, his gaze a conqueror's, his face rigid. ''You're asking for something you may not be able to handle,'' he said quietly. It was a warning.

She swallowed. ''Would you...hurt me?'' she whispered.

He nodded slowly. ''Very probably,'' he said, letting his dark eyes fall to the perfect symmetry of her breasts. ''I've gone a long time without a woman and I'm not particularly gentle even when I haven't. You don't have a lot of experience with men." His eyes shot back up, catching her surprise. "That surprises you? Didn't you know that sophistication is hard to fake?" He smiled gently. "You're blushing. You had to fight not to cover yourself when I looked at you. You're still fighting your primary instinct, which is to turn and run away before I give you what you think you want."

"What I think I want?" she asked in a shaky whisper.

He reached out and the backs of his fingers brushed very lightly over one taut nipple in a blatant, deliberate caress.

She gasped and jerked away, and his eyes reflected the smile on his firm lips.

"You see?" he asked softly. "You'd give yourself to me, with a little coaxing. But not in cold blood. You aren't used to this kind of intimacy with a man."

She did follow her instincts then, and folded her arms over her breasts, shivering as she lowered her eyes to his shirt.

"Twenty-seven. And so inhibited." He sighed heavily. "What happened, Jenny? Was the first time so traumatic that you didn't have the nerve to try again?"

"You don't have the right to ask me questions like that...."

He caught her by the shoulders. "You offered yourself to me," he said curtly. "That gives me the right. Was the first time difficult?"

She couldn't tell him that there hadn't been a first time. That was just too humiliating. "Difficult enough," she said unsteadily. "Please... I'm sorry. I'd like to go in, now."

It was what he'd guessed. She was probably afraid of being with a man intimately because some man had hurt her. It irritated him to think of someone hurting her. He wouldn't have. His hands stilled on her upper arms, feeling the silky warmth of them. He hesitated. He wanted her like hell, but his mind was in control—just barely.

With a rough sigh, he picked her up suddenly and carried her slowly back into the tent, his eyes holding hers. He laid her down gently on her sleeping bag and sat beside her, frowning at the way she crossed her arms over her breasts.

"Don't," he said softly, and moved her arms back to her sides. "Don't cover yourself. Let me look at you. God knows, that's all I can do now."

"You said you didn't want me...." she whispered.

He sighed heavily, his expression sterner than ever, his dark eyes intent on hers. "Yes, I said it. My God, don't you have instincts about men? Don't you know..." He stopped, suddenly aware of the unblinking fascination of her eyes on his face.

Her blond hair was spread around her flushed face in glorious disarray, her small waist and flat stomach faintly visible where her shorts were a little large in the waistline. But he didn't touch her, yet. Only his eyes did, very slowly, very thoroughly, and she trembled all over from just that.

"You're helpless when I look at you," he said quietly. "When I touch you. Is there anything you'd deny me?"

She shook her head slowly, beyond denial. Her body trembled. "But you don't want to make love to me, do you?" she whispered.

"I can't," he said evasively. It wouldn't do to let her know how badly he did want her. His hand went out and she shivered with anticipation, but it was her hair he touched and nothing else, smoothing it away from her face. "I'm not prepared."

"Prepared?" she echoed the word blankly.

He wrapped a strand of blond hair around his forefinger and tugged it gently. "I could make you pregnant," he said simply. "Making love is one thing. Making a baby is something else. It shouldn't happen because two people are careless."

"No," she agreed. She couldn't tell him that to her it wouldn't be careless, that she wanted him and she wanted his child. Loved him, deathlessly. She felt warm all over. Her body arched gently, inviting his eyes. "Oh, please, couldn't you . . . ?" she whispered brokenly.

His breath came jerkily. His eyes slid down her, lingering on her taut nipples. "You ache for me, don't you?" he asked, and there was a kind of bitter compassion in the words.

"So . . . much," she whispered mindlessly. "More than you'll ever know!"

His jaw clenched. She was every man's dream, lying there like that. She was his dream, surely, and it took every ounce of willpower he possessed to hold back.

Despite the hurting tautness of his body, the fever in his blood, he controlled the urge. He bent and gently brushed his lips against hers in the soft stillness of the tent. "Go to sleep," he whispered.

"Hunter," she moaned, her body on fire. Her arms locked around his strong neck, trembling, her eyes frantic. "Please!"

He groaned. "Jenny, you don't understand . . . God!" His mouth opened and crushed down on hers suddenly, and he allowed himself the pleasure of one long, endless kiss. His lips twisted against hers, his chest levered down over her bare breasts. He could feel them through the thin fabric of his shirt, the nipples biting into his skin and he shivered with reaction. She smelled of flowers. Her arms held him, her fingers in his thick, dark hair, caressing him.

His hands slid under her bare back and brought her even closer, his tongue starting to probe her lips. She stiffened, surprising him, because her ardor had been so headlong and eager.

He lifted his dark head, breathing unsteadily. "Don't you like deep kisses?" he asked huskily.

"I . . . I didn't," she said, her own voice shaking. "Not with anyone else." She moved her fingers down to his mouth and touched it hesitantly. "Could you...teach me how?" she breathed at his lips.

The words kindled something explosive in him. It glittered in his eyes. "Yes," he said roughly. "I can teach you."

She was as close to heaven as she'd ever dreamed of being. His mouth bit hers gently, lifting and probing, delicately coaxing. His breath became ragged, and so did hers. He heard her soft gasp as his tongue probed her lips softly, felt her fingers tangle, trembling, in his thick hair.

"Are you ready for me?" he whispered deeply, and felt her shiver. "Open your mouth, and I'll let you feel me . . . inside you."

She cried out. The sound of her voice, the eager parting of her lips sent him over some vague precipice. He groaned, too, as his tongue penetrated her roughly, deeply, in thrusts that lifted her against him and made her weep with reaction. He made a sound deep in his throat and for feverish seconds, he gave her the weight of his body, the unrestrained ardor of his devouring mouth. His hands slid over her bare, silky back, feeling the warm softness of it with blind pleasure, savored the trembling hunger of her mouth. But then he became slowly aware of her uncontrollable shivering, felt the tears in his mouth. Her very abandon was what brought him to his senses. God, what was he doing?

He dragged himself away and sat up, ripping her hands away from his head, her wrists turning white under the involuntary pressure of his lean, dark fingers.

"No!" he said fiercely.

She looked at him through a sensual daze, her eyes smoky with desire, her face expressionless with it. "Hunter," she whispered weakly.

His hands tightened. "I'm Apache," he said harshly. "You're white. My God, don't you understand? We belong to different worlds. This whole damned situation is impossible, Jennifer!"

She realized belatedly that he'd stopped. Her mouth throbbed from the drugging contact with his, and she only began to realize how close he'd come to losing control. So had she. He'd wanted her for those brief seconds, and she gloried in the way he was loving her until he came to his senses. She looked at him hungrily, loving him, awash in sweet pleasure.

"Do you hear me?" he asked, his voice a little less cutting. "Jenny?"

"Yes, I . . . hear you." She caught her breath, her eyes searching over his dark face. "I can't stop shaking," she whispered, surprised by the reactions of her body—new reactions, although he wouldn't realize that. She was a newcomer to raging, abandoned desire. "Oh...my!" she whispered, moaning a little with frustration.

"Shhh," he whispered. His voice sounded actually gentle. "I know. It hurts. But I can't take the risk." He brought her hands to his mouth before he put them down and gently pulled the sleeping bag over her taut breasts, covering her. She was crying. He bent and kissed away the tears, his lips tender on her wet face. "Breathe deeply, little one. It will pass."

He moved away and she watched him through her tears. "My things," she remembered. "I left them by the stream."

"I'll get them." He looked back at her. "I'm going to have a cup of coffee before I come to bed. Do us both a favor and try to be asleep when I come back," he added quietly. "This was a moment out of time, this whole damned trip. But reality is waiting back in Tulsa, and we've got a job to do here. Let's try to get it done and put this behind us."

She swallowed, tugging the sleeping bag closer around her. "You're right, of course," she managed shyly, embarrassed now that her heated skin had cooled. She couldn't meet his eyes. "I'm sorry about what . . . what I did. I . . . I can't think what came over me . . ."

He could feel her embarrassment. Odd, that, when she was twenty-seven and so beautiful. But she'd admitted herself that she'd been hurt, and it had been a long time for her. "Abstinence," he replied. "I know how it feels. You get to the point where you can't bear it any longer. I don't think less of you for wanting me, Jennifer," he added quietly. "I'm rather flattered," he confessed.

She relaxed a little. At least he wasn't ridiculing her. He couldn't know that her abstinence had been lifelong. And through it all, despite that shattering tenderness he'd shown her, he'd kept his head. He said she was beautiful, and he'd looked at her and kissed her. But he knew how badly she'd wanted him, so it might just have been pity. She didn't want to think about that, it hurt too much. She stared at him with soft, quiet eyes.

"How long has it been for you?" she asked gently. "Is it all right, if I ask you that?"

He drew in a slow breath, his broad chest lifting and falling, making his muscles ripple. "Two years," he said.

She searched his hard face. "Is it because I'm white that you won't take the risk?" she asked, her voice barely above a whisper. She had to know.

He stared at her for a long moment. Better to end it here, and temptation with it. "Yes," he said. "I want no possibility, ever, of a child coming from my desire for a woman with white skin."

Desire. Only desire, she thought miserably, and he'd just admitted it. She felt shamed, somehow. "Desire," she whispered.

He schooled his features not to give him away. He nodded his head, very slowly. "Isn't that what you felt for me?" He turned away. "I'll check the perimeter. Good night, Jennifer."

It would have hurt less if he'd hit her, but she didn't say a word. She lay down and closed her eyes. So now she knew. He felt nothing for her, nothing at all, except a desire that was so mild it couldn't even affect his control. And no way was he going to risk the possibility of creating a child. And she wanted nothing more, because she loved him. What a laugh!

Jenny shivered with mingled shame and bitter disappointment. It might have been better if he'd never touched her at all. She wouldn't be able to forget the expert touch of his hands, his mouth, the things he'd whispered to her. He was no novice, and now she was going to spend years remembering that. Tormenting herself with what might have been.

Jenny got up and managed to get another blouse from her suitcase and put it on. Her breasts were still sensitive from the rough contact with his chest. For such a torrid interlude, it had been remarkably innocent, she thought. He'd looked at her, he'd kissed her. But there had been no deep intimacy at all. Because he didn't want her enough, she supposed, and forced her eyes to close.

Outside, Hunter was lighting a cigarette. Smoking might calm his nerves. He looked at the hand holding the cigarette and watched it shake. Jennifer unclothed was a sight to do that to a stronger man than himself. He wondered how he'd ever managed to let her go. His body was burning and throbbing with need of her. She wanted him. He could go back into that tent right now and she'd open her arms for him.

But it would be a mistake. Despite her blatant desire for him, she was somehow less experienced than he'd expected. Shy and even a little afraid, but so hungry for him. He remembered her voice, whispering to him to teach her about deep kisses, the sight of her breasts in the light of the camp fire...

He groaned out loud. Another beauty. Another white woman. She wanted him because he was someone out of her experience, and he'd better remember that. He'd already had a taste of being used for his uniqueness. Jennifer was beautiful enough to choose her own man. He couldn't believe that she'd keep him for long, once her desire was satisfied. Hilarious, really. It was usually the man who pressed the woman for physical satisfaction. Now he was the hunted, and Jennifer the predator. Other men might take what she offered. He couldn't. There was more to it than physical desire. He respected her, as a woman, as a scientist, as a person. He couldn't use her, even without the cultural barriers separating them. But it didn't make the night any easier for him. When he finally gave in to sleep, it was almost dawn.

Jennifer forced herself to work the next two days without thinking back. Hunter himself managed to keep his

mind on his job, scouting the periphery, watching for
signs of interest as they moved camp twice more. He
hadn't been unkind, either. But his attitude toward her
was suddenly impersonal. Employee to employee, with no
personal comments of any kind. Only once, when she
caught him staring at the stream where he'd seen her
bathing, did any emotion show in his lean, hard face. She
pretended not to see, because her own control was pre-
carious. She wanted him still, now more than ever.

Because of that, she pushed herself, working at break-
neck speed to do the samples of the outcrops and decide
where seismic tests would have to be made by the geolog-
ical technicians. Sound technology was the oilman's best
friend, because it could save him millions by telling him
where to drill. It was of the same benefit to the miner.
Modern technology was invaluable when it came to de-
termining underground mineral locations.

In no time, Jennifer had her fieldwork done and was
ready to go back to Tulsa, back to sanity. It was almost a
relief to have temptation out of the way, not to be alone
with Hunter anymore, even if her heart was breaking at
the thought of never having the experience again.

Hunter had registered her silence, her withdrawal. He'd
thanked God for it during the past few days, because his
desire for her had grown beyond bearing. Lying beside her
in the tent at night had kept him sleepless. All he could
think about was the way she'd looked in the firelight, the
sweet vulnerability in her eyes when she'd offered herself
to him, the ardent sweetness of her mouth under his. He
wished he could forget. He had a feeling the memory was
going to haunt him until he died. But if she even remembered what had happened, she gave no indication of it.
She wouldn't look him in the eye anymore, as if her behavior had shamed her. He hated doing that to her, mak-

ing her ashamed of such glorious abandon. But he couldn't give in. He'd fought his own need and won. But it was a hollow victory.

"Glad to be going home?" he asked when they were on the plane.

It was the first remark he'd made in two days that wasn't related to the job.

"Yes," she said without looking at him. "I'm glad."

"That makes two of us," he said with a rough sigh. "Thank God we can get back to normal now."

Normal, she thought, as if her life would ever be that again. Now that she knew his ardor, she knew the touch and feel and taste of him, she was going to starve to death without him. But he seemed completely unaffected by what had happened. And why not? He was experienced. Probably these interludes were part of his work background, and the encounter they'd had was a fairly innocent one. She shivered, thinking what might have happened if he'd wanted her back, if he'd been prepared. She'd never have gotten over him if they'd gone that far. She closed her eyes and tried to sleep. They'd be back in Tulsa soon, and they wouldn't be doing any more traveling together, thank God.

That peaceful thought lasted only until she was sitting in Eugene's office, giving her report. The land containing the potential moly strike was dead on government land, and Eugene cursed roundly.

"They're trading that tract. Look here," he muttered, showing her the area on the map. "They're trading it for a tract they like in Vermont. Damn! All right, there's only one thing to do. Pack an evening gown and some nice clothes. You and Cynthia and I are going to Washington to do some quick lobbying with one of our senators. I went to school with him and he's very Oklahoma-minded. Don't just sit there. Get going! I'll want to leave first thing in the morning.''

''Yes, sir.'' She went home and packed. So much for her idea of staying at home for a while so that she could get over Hunter.

And there was one more unpleasant surprise waiting. When she got to the airport, to board Eugene's corporate jet, who should be waiting with Eugene and his blond wife, Cynthia, but Hunter, looking as irritated and put out as she felt.

Six

Cynthia saw the flash of antagonism in Hunter's dark eyes as Jennifer approached, and she smiled to herself. "You look lovely, Jennifer," she told the younger woman, and linked her arm with Jennifer's. "Let's get buckled up while they finish the walkabout. How have you been?"

Hunter spared Jennifer one brief glance. His expression was as hard as stone. He'd spent days trying to forget her, and fate had thrown him a real curve today. He wanted to go off into the desert and spend some time alone. Maybe that was the answer, when Eugene could spare him. Maybe civilization was getting to him.

"You're brooding," Eugene muttered, glaring at him. "What's the matter?"

"I was just getting used to peace and quiet," Hunter murmured with a dry smile.

"God help us," Eugene shuddered. "Peace and quiet is for the grave, man. No good for healthy humans. Come on. I'll see if I can light a fire under the pilot."

"Better let him do his job," Hunter cautioned. "More than one plane has gone down because its owner was too impatient for the final check."

Eugene glared at him again, but that level stare intimidated even him. "Okay," he muttered. "Have it your own way."

Hunter smiled at the retreating figure, and all the while he was wondering how he was going to survive being close to Jenny without reaching for her.

The flight seemed to take forever. Hunter alternately read and glared at Jennifer, who pretended not to notice. Things had been so strained between them that she was uncomfortable with him. Her behavior in the desert and his reaction to it embarrassed and inhibited her. She sat with Cynthia, only half listening to the older woman's comments about clothes and Washington society while she wondered how she was going to cope with several days of the stoic Mr. Hunter.

They got off the plane at the airport in Washington at last, and Jennifer was momentarily left behind with Hunter while Eugene and Cynthia paused to check times for the return flight with the pilot.

She didn't know what to say to him. She averted her eyes and stared toward the other planes, with her purse and makeup case clutched tightly in her hand.

Hunter was smoking a cigarette. He glanced down at her impatiently and finally stopped and just stared at her until he made her nervous enough to look up. But when he saw her embarrassment, he was sorry he'd done it.

"Don't make it any harder than it already is," he said, his deep voice slow and terse. "What happened that night was just an interlude. I lost my head and so did you. Let it go."

She swallowed. "All right."

He scowled through a cloud of smoke as he searched her deep blue eyes. Involuntarily his gaze slid to her blouse and his eyes darkened with memories.

She turned away. That look was painful, and despite his assertion that it was over, it didn't seem as if he'd forgotten a single thing. Neither had she. The feel of his eyes on her, his mouth on her lips, haunted her night after lonely night. She didn't even like being near him because just his proximity made her shiver with need. It was a reaction unlike anything she'd ever experienced before in her life, a mad hunger that she could never satisfy.

Hunter was having problems of his own. God, she was lovely! Just looking at her hurt. He turned away to help get the luggage off the plane and carry it to the waiting limousine. He had to stop remembering.

The hotel they stayed at was four-star, very plush and service-oriented. Eugene had reserved two suites of rooms. Unfortunately, Jennifer was relegated to one with Hunter, which surprised and inhibited her.

Eugene noticed her uneasiness and averted his eyes before she could see the faint glimmer of amusement in them. "You'll survive it, Jenny," he said. "I want you where Hunter can watch you. You're the most important part of this enterprise. I can't have enemy agents trying to spirit you off under my nose, can I?"

"We have other security people...." she began hopefully.

"But Hunter's the best. No more arguments. I hope you brought an evening gown. There's an embassy ball tomorrow night."

"I did," she said reluctantly. It was a year old, but still functional, and it fit her like a second skin. She frowned bitterly, thinking of the exquisite white confection and regretting that she didn't still have the little red number she'd knocked Hunter's eyes out with a few months back. She'd thrown it away in a temper after that one bitter date with him.

Eugene had arranged appointments all over Washington, and he went alone, leaving Jennifer to go sightseeing with Cynthia and Hunter.

Cynthia was enchanted with everything she saw, from the Lincoln Memorial to the reflecting pool outside it, the spire of the Washington monument and the White House and the nation's Capital. But Jennifer was enchanted with Hunter and trying so hard not to let him see. She wore tan slacks with a colorful pink blouse and sandals for the sight-seeing tour, and Cynthia wore a similar ensemble. Hunter wore a suit.

He escorted them around the city with quiet impatience, and Jennifer knew without being told that he hated the noise and traffic, and that he would have preferred to be doing something else. But he didn't complain. He pointed out landmarks and hustled them in and out of cabs with singular forbearance. All the same, Jennifer noticed how relieved he looked when they were back at the hotel.

Eugene returned in time to go to supper, phoning Hunter to give him the time and place they were to eat. Hunter hung up, glancing at a nervous Jennifer poised in the doorway to her bedroom.

"You've got an hour to get dressed," he said. "Time for a shower, if you like. We're to meet him and Cynthia at the Coach and Whip for dinner."

"All right," she said. "I'll be ready."

THE JOKER GOES WILD!

Play
this
card
right!

See
inside!

SILHOUETTE®
WANTS TO <u>GIVE</u> YOU

- 4 free books
- A free gold-plated chain
- A free mystery gift

IT'S A WILD, WILD, WONDERFUL
FREE OFFER!
HERE'S WHAT YOU GET:

1. *Four New Silhouette Desire® Novels—FREE!*
   Everything comes up hearts and diamonds with four exciting romances—yours FREE from Silhouette Reader Service™. Each of these brand-new novels brings you the passion and tenderness of today's greatest love stories.

2. *A Lovely and Elegant Gold-Plated Chain—FREE!*
   You'll love your elegant 20k gold electroplated chain! The necklace is finely crafted with 160 double-soldered links and is electroplate finished in genuine 20k gold. And it's yours free as added thanks for giving our Reader Service a try!

3. *An Exciting Mystery Bonus—FREE!*
   You'll go wild over this surprise gift. It is attractive as well as practical.

4. *Convenient Home Delivery!*
   Join Silhouette Reader Service™ and enjoy the convenience of previewing six new books every month, delivered to your home. Each book is yours for $2.24*—26¢ less than the cover price—plus only 69¢ delivery for the entire shipment! If you're not fully satisfied, you can cancel at any time, just by sending us a note or a shipping statement marked "cancel" or by returning any shipment to us at our cost. Great savings and total convenience are the name of the game at Silhouette!

5. *Free Newsletter!*
   It makes you feel like a partner to the world's most popular authors . . . tells about their upcoming books . . . even gives you their recipes!

6. *More Mystery Gifts Throughout the Year! No joke!*
   Because home subscribers are our most valued readers, we'll be sending you additional free gifts from time to time with your monthly shipments—as a token of our appreciation!

GO WILD
WITH SILHOUETTE® TODAY—
JUST COMPLETE, DETACH AND
MAIL YOUR FREE-OFFER CARD!

*Terms and prices subject to change without notice.
© 1990 HARLEQUIN ENTERPRISES LIMITED

GET YOUR GIFTS FROM SILHOUETTE®
ABSOLUTELY FREE!

Mail this card today!

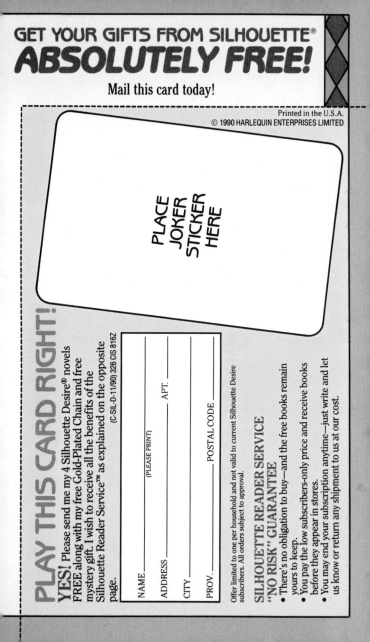

PLACE
JOKER
STICKER
HERE

PLAY THIS CARD RIGHT!

YES! Please send me my 4 Silhouette Desire® novels FREE along with my free Gold-Plated Chain and free mystery gift. I wish to receive all the benefits of the Silhouette Reader Service™ as explained on the opposite page.

(C-SIL-D-11/90) 326 CIS 8162

NAME _____
(PLEASE PRINT)

ADDRESS _____ APT. _____

CITY _____

PROV. _____ POSTAL CODE _____

Offer limited to one per household and not valid to current Silhouette Desire subscribers. All orders subject to approval.

SILHOUETTE READER SERVICE "NO RISK" GUARANTEE

- There's no obligation to buy—and the free books remain yours to keep.
- You pay the low subscribers-only price and receive books before they appear in stores.
- You may end your subscription anytime—just write and let us know or return any shipment to us at our cost.

IT'S NO JOKE!

**MAIL THE POSTPAID CARD AND
GET FREE GIFTS AND $10.00 WORTH OF
SILHOUETTE NOVELS—FREE!**

If offer card is missing, write to:
Silhouette Reader Service, P.O. Box 609, Fort Erie, Ontario L2A 5X3

**Business
Reply Mail**

No Postage Stamp
Necessary if Mailed
in Canada

Postage will be paid by

**SILHOUETTE
READER SERVICE
P.O. BOX 609
FORT ERIE, ONTARIO
L2A 9Z9**

Canada Post
Postes Canada
125

He stared at her with quiet, steady dark eyes. "What are you going to wear?"

"Why?" she asked, startled.

He pursed his lips. "I hope it isn't something red," he murmured, turning away with an involuntary smile on his hard mouth.

"Oh!" she burst out.

But, he didn't look back or say a word. He just went into his own room and closed the door.

Except for that one unexpected incident, dinner went off without a hitch. But if she'd hoped for anything from Hunter, she was doomed for disappointment. He ate and excused himself, and she didn't see him again for the rest of the night or most of the next day. She and Cynthia amused themselves by going to a movie while Eugene had one last talk with someone on Capitol Hill. Then, almost before she knew it, Jennifer was getting ready to go to a real ball.

Jennifer felt like a girl on her first date as she put on the white satin gown to wear to the ball. She'd never been to anything really grand, although she'd come close once when she and Hunter were on assignment overseas. She put her long blond hair up in an elegant coiffure with tiny wisps of hair curling around her ears. She had a pair of satin-covered pumps that she wore with it, but the dress itself was the height of expensive luxury. She'd bought it on impulse, because at the time she'd had no place at all to wear it. It had a low-cut bodice and spaghetti straps that tied on each shoulder. The waist was fitted, but the skirt had yards and yards of material, and it flared gracefully when she walked. It covered all but the very tips of her pumps. She put on her makeup last, using just a little more than she usually did, but not too much. She looked in the mirror, fascinated because she looked totally different this way. Her whole face seemed radiant with the extra touch of rouge and the pale gray eye shadow with a tiny hint of light blue.

She looked at herself with faint satisfaction. She'd never been glad of her looks before, but tonight she was. She wanted Hunter to be proud of her, to want to be seen with her. She closed her eyes, imagining the music of a waltz. Would Hunter ask her to dance? She smiled. Surely he would. They'd waltz around the ballroom and all eyes would be on them . . . That jerked her back to reality. Attention would be the last thing Hunter would want, and probably the only dances he knew were done with war dances around a camp fire.

She grimaced mentally. That would be just the thing to say to him, all right. It would put them quickly back on their old, familiar footing and he'd never speak to her again. Which might not be a bad idea, she told herself. At least if he hated her openly he wouldn't be making horrible remarks about the red dress she'd worn that one evening they'd gone out together.

On the other hand, why had he mentioned it at all? That was twice, she realized, that he'd made a remark about that particular dress. She smiled to herself. Well, well. He remembered it, did he? She'd go right out and find herself another red dress, one that was even more revealing, and she'd wear it until he screamed!

The sudden hard rap on the door made her jump. "Yes?" she called out.

"Time to go," Hunter replied quietly.

She grabbed her purse, almost upending the entire contents on the floor in the process, and rushed to their joint sitting room.

She stopped short at the sight of Hunter in a dinner jacket. It could have been made for him, she thought as she stared at him. The dark jacket with its white silk shirt and black tie might have been designed for his coloring. It made him look so elegant and handsome that she couldn't tear her eyes away.

He was doing some looking of his own. His dark eyes ran down the length of her body in the clinging white dress, growing narrower and glittering faintly as they lingered on her full breasts and worked their way back up to her soft mouth and then her dark blue eyes.

"Will I do?" she asked hesitantly.

"You'll do," he said, his voice terse with reluctant emotion. He met her eyes and held them, watching her cheeks go pink. "Oh, yes, you'll do, Jennifer. And you know it without having to be told."

She dragged her gaze down to his chest, to the quick rise and fall of it under the shirt. "You don't have to sound angry," she muttered.

"I am angry. You know it. And don't pretend you don't know why. I wouldn't buy that in a million years." He moved toward the door while she was still trying to puzzle out what he meant. "Let's go," he said, without looking at her again. "Eugene and Cynthia are waiting for us."

She started past him and paused without knowing why. Slowly she lifted her eyes to his and looked at him openly. Her heart ran wild at the fierce warmth she saw there, at the visible effort he made at control. "Is it all right if I tell you that you're devastating?" she asked softly.

He lifted his chin without replying, but something flashed in his dark eyes for an instant before he turned away with a faint smile. "Come on."

He was quiet when they joined the other couple, which was just as well, because Eugene monopolized the conversation—as usual. It was exciting to go to a ball in a big black limousine, and Jennifer wished her parents could see her now. She almost looked up at Hunter and said so, but he wouldn't find it interesting, she knew, so she kept her silence.

The big Washington mansion where the ball was being held was some embassy or other. Jennifer had been too excited about being with Hunter to care which one it was, or even where it was. She was trembling with contained excitement when Hunter helped her from the car and escorted her up the wide steps that led to the columned porch, which was ablaze with light. The faint sounds of music poured from the stately confines of the mansion.

"What a piece of real estate," Cynthia said mischievously, clasping Eugene's hand tightly in her own. "And I thought we had a nice house."

"We do have a nice house," he reminded her. "And we could have had one like this, but you seemed to think that it would be—what was the word you used?—pretentious."

"And it would have," she reassured him. "I was just admiring the pretentiousness of the embassy," she added, tongue-in-cheek.

Jennifer grinned. "Do you suppose the staff wear roller skates to get from room to room with the trays?"

"I wouldn't be a bit surprised," Eugene said, "but for God's sake don't make such a remark to our host. You can take it from me that he has absolutely no sense of humor."

"Can I ask why we're going to a ball at a foreign embassy to talk about land out West?" Jennifer asked.

"Sure!" Eugene assured her.

She glared at him.

He chuckled. "All right. There are two senators I have to see, and I was tipped off that they were both going to be at this shindig. You and Hunter go socialize until I need you—if I need you. I may be be able to pull this one off alone."

"Then why are we here?" Jennifer persisted.

Eugene forcibly kept himself from glancing at Hunter. "Because I wanted to make sure you weren't abducted and held for ransom or some such thing while I was talking terms," he said. "Go and dance. Can you dance?" he taunted.

She drew herself up to her full height, an action that made her firm breasts thrust out proudly, and Hunter shifted a little jerkily and moved away. "Yes, I can dance," she told him. "In fact, I studied dancing for three years."

"So go and practice." His blue eyes narrowed on Hunter's averted face. "You might teach Hunter how."

Hunter cocked a thick eyebrow down at him. "My people could teach yours plenty about how to move to music." A wisp of a smile touched that hard face and his dark eyes twinkled. "We have dances for war, dances for peace, dances for rain, even dances for fertility," he added and had to grit his teeth to keep from glancing deliberately toward Jennifer.

"How about waltzes?" Eugene persisted.

"Ballroom dancing isn't included in the core curriculum for CIA operatives," he said, deadpan.

"Jennifer might be persuaded to teach you..." Eugene began.

But before he could even get the words out, Jennifer was suddenly swept away by a tall, balding man with a badge of office on the sash that arrowed across his thin chest. She was dancing before she knew it, and from that moment on, she didn't even get a peek at the hors d'oeuvres on the long, elegant table against the wall. She was dying of thirst, too, but one partner after another asked her to dance, and she was too entranced by the exquisite music of the live orchestra to refuse. Especially since Hunter didn't even bother to ask her for a dance, whether or not he knew how. When her first partner swept her off onto the dance floor, he'd walked away without even looking back and she hadn't seen him since.

She pleaded fatigue after a nonstop hour on the dance floor and found her way to the powder room upstairs. By the time she came down, Hunter had apparently come out of hiding because an older socialite had him cornered by a potted plant against one wall. He looked irritated and half angry, and Jennifer felt a surge of sympathy, although God alone knew why she should.

She started toward him, hesitated, and he looked up at that moment and his eyes kindled. He even smiled.

That had to mean he was desperate for rescue. He never smiled at her. Well, he was going to get his rescue, but she was going to enjoy it. She moved toward him with pure witchery in her movements, patting her hair back into place.

"Here I am, sweetheart!" she called in a rich exaggerated Southern drawl. "Did you think I'd gotten lost?" She draped herself over his side, feeling him stiffen. A mischievous sense of pleasure flooded through her. Well, he'd asked for it. She smiled thinly at the older woman, who was watching her with narrow, cold eyes. "Hello. I don't think we've met. I'm Jennifer Marist. Hunter and I work for an oil corporation in Oklahoma. It's so rarely that we get to enjoy a fabulous party like this, isn't it, darling?" she asked, blinking her long lashes up at him.

"Rarely," he agreed, but his eyes were promising retribution. He was already half out of humor from watching her pass from one pair of masculine arms to another.

Then this social shark had attacked. He'd been desperate enough to encourage Jennifer to rescue him, but he hadn't exactly expected this type of rescue. Fortunately his expression gave nothing away.

"I was just telling Mr. Hunter that I'd love to have him join me for a late supper," the older woman said, blatantly ignoring Jennifer's apparent possessiveness. She smiled at Hunter, diamonds dripping from her ears and her thin neck. "I want to hear all about his tribe. I've never met a real Indian before."

Hunter's jaw clenched, but Jennifer smiled.

"I know, isn't it fascinating?" Jennifer confided. "Did you know that he rubs himself all over with bear grease every night at bedtime? It's a ritual. And he keeps rattlesnakes," she whispered, "to use in fertility dances outside during full moons. You really must get him to show you the courting dance. It's done with deer heads and pouches full of dried buffalo chips...."

The older woman was looking a little frantic. "Excuse me," she said breathlessly, staring around as if she were looking for a life preserver. "I see someone I must speak to!"

She shot off without another word and Jennifer had to smother a giggle. "Oh, God, I'm sorry," she whispered. "It was the way she said it..."

He was laughing, too, if the glitter in his eyes and the faint uplift of his lips could be called that. "Bear grease," he muttered. "That wasn't the Apache, you idiot. And the dance a young girl does at her very special coming-of-age ceremony is done with a pouch of pollen, for fertility, not dried buffalo chips."

"Do you want me to call her back and tell her the truth?" she offered.

He shook his head. His dark eyes slid over her body in the clinging dress, and there was a definite appreciation in them. "If I have to suffer a woman for the rest of the evening, I'd prefer you," he said, startling her. "At least you won't ask embarrassing questions about my cultural background."

"Thanks a lot," she murmured. "And after that daring rescue, too."

"Rescue, yes. Daring?" He shook his head. "Hardly." He chuckled deeply. "You little terror. I ought to tie you to a chair and smear honey on you."

"You have to do that in the desert, where you can find ants," she reminded him. "You asked to be rescued, you know you did."

"This wasn't exactly what I had in mind," he muttered.

"Was she trying to put the make on you?" she asked, all eyes.

He glared at her. "No. She was trying to find out how many scalps I had in my teepee."

"Apaches didn't have teepees, they had wickiups," she said knowledgeably. "I hope you told her."

His eyebrows rose. "Who's the Indian here, you or me?"

"I think one of my great-grandfather's adoptive cousins was Lower Creek," she frowned thoughtfully.

"God help us!"

"I could have just kept on walking," she reminded him. "I didn't have to save you from that woman."

"No, you didn't. But before it happens again, I'm going to stand on the balcony and hope I get carried off by Russian helicopters. I hate these civilized hatchet parties."

"Mind if I join you?" she asked.

His eyes narrowed. "What for? You're the belle of the ball. You've danced every damned dance!"

"Only because you walked off and left me alone!" she threw back at him, her blue eyes flashing. "I thought we were together. But I suppose that's carrying the line of duty too far, isn't it? I mean, God forbid you should have to survive a whole evening in my company!"

"I said I was going outside," he replied with exaggerated patience. "If you want to come along, fine. I don't like being the only Indian around. Where were all these damned suicidal white women over a hundred years ago? I'll tell you, they were hiding behind curtains with loaded rifles! But now, all of a sudden, they can't wait to be thrown on a horse and carried off."

"You're shouting," she pointed out.

His dark eyes glittered down at her. "I am not," he said shortly.

"Besides, you don't have a horse."

"I have one at home," he replied. "Several, in fact. I like horses."

"So do I. But I haven't ridden much," she replied. "There was never much time for that sort of thing."

"People make time for the things they really want to do," he said, looking down at her.

She shrugged. "There are plenty of places to ride around Tulsa, but I think it's a mistake to get on a horse if you don't know how to control it."

"Well, well." He stood aside to let her precede him onto the balcony, past the colorful blur of dancing couples. The balcony was dark and fairly deserted, with huge potted plants and trees and a balustrade that overlooked the brilliant lights of the city.

Seven

Jennifer couldn't believe he'd actually allowed her to invade his solitude without a protest. It was sheer heaven being here beside him on the balcony, without another soul in sight.

She leaned forward on the balustrade. "Isn't it glorious?" she asked softly.

He studied her hungrily for a moment before he turned his gaze toward the horizon. "I prefer sunset on the desert." He lit a cigarette and smoked it silently for several seconds before his dark eyes cut sideways to study her. "Did you really want to dance with me?" he asked with a faint smile. Actually he danced quite well. But having Jenny close was a big risk. She went to his head even when they were several feet apart.

"Wasn't it obvious that I did?" she asked ruefully.

"Not to me." He blew out a cloud of smoke and stared at the distant horizon. "I won't dance, Jennifer. Not this kind of dancing, anyway.'' He was careful to say *won't* and not *can't*—lying was almost impossible for him. Apaches considered it bad manners to lie.

''Oh. I'm sorry. You do everything else so well, I just assumed that dancing would come naturally to you.''

''It doesn't,'' he replied. ''Where did you learn?''

''Dancing class,'' she said, grinning. Odd how comfortable she felt with him, despite the feverish excitement his closeness engendered in her slender body. She could catch the scent of his cologne, and it was spicy and sexy in her nostrils. He was the stuff dreams were made of. Her dreams, anyway.

''You studied ballroom dancing?'' he persisted.

''Tap and ballet, actually. My mother thought I should be well-rounded instead of walking around with my nose stuck in a book or studying rocks most of the time.''

''What are your parents like?'' he asked, curious.

She smiled, picturing them. ''My mother looks like me. My father's tall and very dark. They're both educators and I think they're nice people. Certainly they're intelligent.''

''They'd have to be, with such a brainy daughter.''

She laughed self-consciously. ''I'm not brainy really. I had to study pretty hard to get where I am.'' She smiled wistfully.

''You know your job,'' he replied, glancing down at her. ''I learned more about molybdenum than I wanted to know.''

She blushed. ''Yes, well, I tend to ramble sometimes.''

''It wasn't a criticism,'' he said. ''I enjoyed it.'' He looked out over the horizon. ''God, I hate society.''

''I guess it gets difficult for you when people start making insulting remarks about your heritage,'' she said. ''It's hard for me when I get dragged on the dance floor

by men I don't even know. I don't particularly like being
handled.''

He frowned. He hadn't thought of her beauty as being
a handicap. Maybe it was. She'd had enough partners tonight. Enough, in fact, to make him jealous for the first
time in memory.

"I don't like being an oddity," he agreed. "I've never
thought of you that way."

She smiled. "Thank you. I could return the compli-
ment."

He turned away from her, leaning against the balcony
to look out at the city lights. "I suppose I'm less easily
offended than I was before you joined the company.
Maybe I'm learning to take that chip off my shoulder,"
he added, glancing at her with a rueful smile. "Isn't that
what you once accused me of having?"

She joined him by the balcony, leaning her arms on it.
"Yes. It was true. You got your back up every time I made
a remark."

"You intimidated me," he said surprisingly. He lifted
the cigarette to his firm lips, glancing down at her.
"Beautiful, blond, intelligent . . . the kind of woman who
could have any man she wanted. I didn't think a reservation Indian would appeal to you."

"I suppose you got the shock of your life that night by
the creek," she remarked, a little shy at the admission.

"Indeed I did," he said huskily. His eyes darkened. "I
never dreamed you wanted me like that."

"It wasn't enough, though," she said sadly, her eyes
moving to the dark landscape. "Wanting on one side, I
mean." She pushed back a loose strand of blond hair that
had escaped her elegant upswept coiffure. "You didn't
smoke while we were camping out."

"You didn't see me," he corrected. "It's my only vice, and just an occasional one. I have the infrequent can of beer, but I don't drink." His eyes narrowed. "Alcoholism is a big problem among my people. Some scientists have ventured the opinion that Indians lack the enzyme necessary to process alcohol."

"I didn't know. I don't drink, either. I like being in control of my senses."

"Do you?" He looked down at her quietly.

She wouldn't meet his eyes. "I always have been. Except with you."

He sighed angrily, lifting the cigarette to his mouth again before he ground it out under his heel. "So I noticed," he said gruffly. Her nearness was making him uncomfortable. He didn't like the temptation of being close to her, but he didn't want to spoil the evening for her by saying so.

She moved a little closer so that she could see his lean, dark face in the light from the ballroom. "Hunter, what's wrong?" she asked softly.

He hated the tenderness in her voice. It tempted him and made him angry. "Nothing."

She wanted to pursue the subject, but his expression was daunting. She smoothed down the soft material of the dress. With its sleeveless bodice that dipped almost to her waist, and the clingy chiffon outlining her narrow waist and full hips, she was a vision. She knew she looked pretty, but it would have made her evening to hear Hunter say so. Not that he would. She glanced back toward the dancers inside. "I guess this is familiar territory to you," she murmured absently. "High society, I mean."

He frowned. "I beg your pardon?"

"Well, you do a lot of work for Eugene, and this is his milieu," she explained, glancing up at him. "And I know you've had to look after politicians for him, so I suppose it entails a certain amount of socializing."

"Not that much." He folded his arms over his chest. "I don't care for this kind of civilized warfare. Too many people. Too much noise."

"I know how you feel." She sighed, staring toward the ballroom. "I'd much rather be outdoors, away from crowds."

He studied her with renewed interest. She wasn't lying. He remembered her delight in the desert those days they'd spent together, her laughter at the antics of the birds, her quiet contemplation of dusk and dawn. That pleasure hadn't been faked. But with her beauty and education, surely this was her scene.

"You look at home here, nevertheless," he said. He lit another cigarette and blew out a cloud of smoke. She was making him more nervous by the minute. Her dress was pure witchcraft.

"That's funny," she murmured, and smiled. "The closest to this kind of thing I ever got in my youth was the high school prom—or it would have been, if I'd been asked. I spent that night at home, baby-sitting the neighbor's little boy."

The cigarette froze en route to his mouth. "You weren't asked?"

"You sound surprised." She turned to look up at him. "All the boys assumed that I already had a date, because I was pretty. There was one special boy I liked, but he was just ordinary and not handsome at all. He didn't think he had a chance with me, so he never asked me out. I didn't find out until I was grown and he was married that he'd had a crush on me." She laughed, but it had a hollow sound. "Women hate me because they think I'm a threat to them. Men don't take me seriously at work if they don't know me because pretty blondes aren't supposed to be intelligent. And if I'm asked out on a date, it's automatically expected that I'll be dynamite in bed. You mentioned once that I don't date anybody. Now you know why."

"Are you?" he asked.

Her eyebrows lifted. "Am I what?"

"Dynamite in bed."

She glared up at him. There was something like amusement in his tone. "Don't you start, Hunter."

He tossed the cigarette down and ground it out under the heel of his dress shoe, but his eyes didn't leave hers. "Why not?" he asked, moving closer with a slow sensual step that made her heart beat faster. "I'm human."

"Are you, really?" she asked, remembering that night on the desert when he'd seen her bathing. She almost groaned. His restraint had overwhelmed her, then and since.

He caught her hands and slid them up around his neck. "Stop dithering and dance with me," he said quietly.

His voice was an octave lower. Deep, slow, sensuous, like the hands that, instead of holding her correctly, slid around her, against her bare back where the low cut of the dress left it vulnerable.

She gasped. "You said...you didn't dance," she whispered.

"You can teach me," he whispered back.

But it didn't feel as if he needed any instruction. He moved gracefully to the music, drawing her along with him. The feel of him this close, the brush of his warm, rough hands against her silky skin, made her tremble. When he felt the trembling, he drew her even closer. She shivered helplessly, feeling his hands slowly caressing her, his lips in her hair, against her forehead, as he made a lazy

effort to move her to the rhythm of the slow bluesy tune
the orchestra was playing. But it wasn't as much dancing
as it was making love to music. She felt his chest dragging against her breasts with every step, his long, powerful legs brushing against hers at the thigh. She
remembered his eyes on her bare breasts, his arms around
her, the feel of his hard mouth. And she ached for him.

She tried to move back, before she gave herself away,
but his hands were firm.

"What are you afraid of?" he asked at her forehead.

"You," she moaned. "What you make me feel." Her
hands grasped the lapels of his jacket. Twenty-seven years
of denial, of longing, of loneliness. Years of loving this
man alone, of being deprived of even the most innocent
physical contact. And now she was in his arms, he was
holding her, touching her, and she couldn't hide her pleasure or her need.

"Jenny." He bent closer, his mouth tempting hers into
lifting, his eyes dark and quiet and intent in the stillness.
He stopped dancing, but his hands smoothed lazily up and
down her back, and he watched the rapt, anguished need
color her face, part her lips. She looked as if she'd die to
have him make love to her. It was the same look he remembered from the night he'd seen her bathing, and it
had the same overwhelming effect on him.

"Please," she whispered, and her voice broke. She was
beyond hiding it, beyond pretence, totally vulnerable.
"Would it kill you to kiss me again, just once? Oh, Hunter, please...!"

He lifted his head with a rough sigh, looking around
them. He eased her into a small alcove, hidden to the rest
of the balcony, and slowly moved her until she was against
the wall. His hands rested on either side of her head
against it, his body shielding hers, and then covering hers,

trapping her between it and the wall in a slow, sensual movement.

"Lift your mouth to mine," he whispered.

She did, without a single protest, and had it taken in a succession of slow, brief, tormenting bites. She whimpered helplessly, shaking all over with the need to be close to him. He tasted of cigarette smoke and expensive brandy, and the kiss was almost like a narcotic, drugging her with slow, aching pleasure. She clung to him with something akin to desperation, so out of control that she couldn't begin to hide what she was feeling. Her body throbbed with it, trembled with it. Twenty-seven years of denial were going up in flames, in his arms.

"My God, you're starving for me," he said huskily, his voice rough with surprise as he looked down at her. "It's all right, little one," he breathed as his dark head bent again. "It's all right. I'll feed you . . ."

His mouth covered hers then, slowly building the pressure into something wild and deep and overwhelming. As if he understood her need for passion, he pushed down against her and his mouth became demanding, its very roughness filling the emptiness in her.

She slid her arms around his lean waist and pressed even closer, tears rolling down her flushed cheeks as she fed on his mouth, accepting the hard thrust of his tongue with awe, loving the feel of his aroused body bearing hers heavily against the wall. She wept against his hard lips and he lifted his head.

"Oh, don't . . . stop," she whispered brokenly. "Please, please . . . don't stop yet!"

He was losing it. His mouth ground into hers again, tasting the softness of her parted lips, inhaling the exquisite fragrance of her body into his nostrils. His body was rigid with desire, his hips already thrusting helplessly against hers with an involuntary rhythm. His mouth crushed hers roughly, his teeth nipping her full lower lip in a pagan surge of fierce need.

"I want you," she whispered into his mouth. All her control was gone, all her pride. She was beyond rational thought. "I want you. I want you so much!"

He dragged his head up. His hands gripped her upper arms hard while he fought for control. She'd already lost hers. Her eyes were dilated, wild with need, her body shaking helplessly with it. She was his. Here, now, standing up, she would have welcomed him and he knew it. It was all he could do to back away. But he had to remember who they were, and where they were.

"Jennifer," he said quietly. His voice sounded strained. He fought to steady it. "Jennifer!" He shook her. "Stop it!"

She felt the rough shake as if it was happening to somebody else. She stared up at him through a sensual veil, still shivering, her body throbbing with its urgent need of his. He shook her again, fiercely, and she caught her breath. The world spun around her and she suddenly realized where they were.

She swallowed hard with returning sanity. Her face went scarlet when she remembered begging him...

His hands tightened and released her arms. "Come on, now," he said, his voice gentle where it had been violent. "Come on, Jenny. Take a deep breath."

He knew she was vulnerable. He knew it all now. Tears ran down her cheeks, hot and salty, into the corners of her swollen mouth.

He drew her head to his jacket, his hands soothing at her nape. "It's all right, little one," he said quietly, his teeth clenched as he fought his own physical demons. He was hurting. "It's all right. Nothing happened."

"I want to die," she whispered brokenly. "I'm so...
ashamed!"

"Of what?" he asked, frowning. He framed her face in
his lean, warm hands and lifted it to his eyes. "Jenny,
there's no shame in being a woman."

She could hardly see him through her tears. "Let me
go... please," she pleaded, pushing at his chest.

He didn't like the way she looked. Desperate. Horri-
fied. As if she'd committed some deadly sin. He couldn't
let her leave in this condition.

"Calm down," he said firmly, taking her by the shoulders to shake her again. "I'm not letting you out of my
sight until you're rational."

She bit down on her swollen lower lip, hard, tasting him
there. She closed her eyes. She couldn't bear to see his
face.

"What in God's name is wrong with you?" he asked,
leaning closer. "You wanted me, that's all. I've felt that
kind of desire before, I know how helpless it can make
you."

Yes, he'd felt it, but not with her. That was what hurt
so much, that she felt it and he didn't. He'd kissed her
because she'd begged him to, but she was sure there hadn't
been anything else. Just pity and compassion. If only she
knew more about men...

She lifted her cold hands and wiped at her tears. "I
need to wash my face," she whispered. "I can't go back
in there... like this."

He bent and brushed his lips tenderly against hers, but
she jerked away from him, her blue eyes wide and terri-
fied.

His head lifted and he studied her, realization kindling
belatedly in his mind. So that was it. The hidden fear.
She'd lost control. He'd made her helpless and she was

going to fight tooth and nail to keep it from happening again. Was that why she didn't date anyone? Had she lost control before and was afraid of giving rein to her passionate nature? Or was it just years of denial catching up with her? Her violent desire for him had weakened his resolve painfully.

"Do you want me to do something about this?" he asked, his voice deep and quiet, posing a question he'd never meant to ask.

"What?" she asked numbly.

"A need that violent should be satisifed," he said matter-of-factly. "I know you want me. I've known that for a long time. But now I understand how desperate the need is."

She couldn't believe he was saying this. Her face was scarlet, she knew, but she stared up at him helplessly while he offered her the fulfillment of every dream she'd ever dreamed.

"Do you want me to take you back to the hotel and satisfy you, Jenny?" he asked quietly, his expression giving away nothing, although his body was still keeping him on the rack. He wanted her obsessively. He could taste her in his mouth. He wanted to taste all of her the way he'd savored her soft lips. He wanted to strip her and kiss every pink inch of her, from head to toe.

"I . . . might get pregnant," she whispered, too shaken to be rational, too hungry to refuse. "You said . . ."

He didn't like remembering what he'd said. "I'll take care of you," he said firmly. "In every way. There won't be consequences of any kind. Least of all the risk of a child torn between your culture and mine," he added bitterly.

She was twenty-seven, almost twenty-eight. She'd never known intimacy with anyone, but she wanted, so much, to know it with this man. She'd loved him forever, it sometimes seemed. He was offering her untold delights. She knew without asking that he was expert. The way he'd kissed her had told her that. He wouldn't hurt her. With luck, he'd never know that she was a virgin.

"I . . . want you," she whispered helplessly.

His chest expanded jerkily while he searched her eyes, curious about the faint fear and melancholy there. But one didn't question a gift like this. He caught her soft hand in his and led her back into the ballroom.

She remembered very little about the minutes that followed. They left. She said something polite to their host and hostess and to Eugene and Cynthia. There was a cab ride back to the hotel, she was at the door of his room. He put her inside without bothering to turn on the light.

Then she was in his arms. It was heaven. Pure, sweet heaven. He took her hair down and buried his face in it before his mouth slowly, inevitably, found her lips. She clung to him, tasting him, while he kissed her and kissed her until she couldn't stand. She felt his mouth and his hands on her bare skin as he removed her dress, her underthings, her hose. Then he lifted her and carried her to the bed.

"I want to look at you," he said huskily.

"Yes." She didn't flinch as the bedside light came on, although her cheeks reddened, even though he'd seen part of her like this before. He looked and she shivered at the bold hunger in his dark eyes as they went over her slowly, with fierce possessiveness.

"Pink satin," he whispered, his voice deep and slow in the stillness of the room. "I wanted to look at you like this that night you were bathing, at all of you. I wanted to touch you, but I didn't dare. I couldn't have stopped." He reached down and spread her hair on his pillow, his eyes darkening. "Exquisite," he whispered, his eyes sliding down her.

She shivered. She hadn't expected him to say things like that.

He sat down beside her, still fully clothed, not touching her. His eyes searched hers. "This is the first time," he said.

Her heart jumped. He knew!

"The first time," he continued, "that I've been with a white woman in years. This is something I never meant to happen."

She couldn't help the relief she felt that he hadn't guessed about her innocence. But what he was saying finally got through to her and she realized what it meant.

"You don't have to," she said uncertainly, because now that it was about to happen, she was nervous.

He reached out and traced one soft, firm breast, watching her body react helplessly and instantly to his touch. "I'm Apache," he said, studying her face. "There are places inside me that you can't see, can't touch. Different beliefs, different customs, different life-styles. I live in your world, but I prefer the stark simplicity of mine." He traced around one dusky erect nipple, hearing her soft gasp. "I've spent years trying not to see you, Jennifer," he said, his voice barely above a whisper. "Years of dreams that kept my body in anguish..." He bent to her breasts, his mouth slow and ardent.

She couldn't believe he'd said that. She shivered and arched toward his lips, holding his face to her. "You mean... you want me, too?" she asked, fascinated.

He lifted his head and looked down into her eyes. "Yes," he said simply. "But only this once," he added, his voice stern. "Only tonight. Never again."

She swallowed. She wanted so much more than that, but it would have to do. She could live on this for the rest of her life. "All right," she whispered.

He stood with a long sigh and began to remove his own clothes. He did it with lazy grace, with a complete lack of inhibition that told her too well how familiar this was to him. She hated the other women in his life because they'd given him that expertise.

His keen eyes caught her expression and he lifted an eyebrow as he bent to remove the final barrier. "What was that hard look about?" he asked.

He turned back to her and the hard look was utterly forgotten as she stared blatantly at his nudity. He was all bronzed muscle and powerful etched lines and curves, so beautiful that she sat up and caught her breath at the perfection of his body.

"What is it?" he asked, frowning curiously.

"There was a statue in the Louvre," she stammered. "I saw photographs of it…Greek, I think. I remember being awed by the power and beauty of it and thinking that, well, that no mortal man could come close to that kind of perfection." She averted her eyes to the bed. "I didn't mean to stare. I guess you've been told ad nauseum how…beautifully masculine you are."

He felt the impact of that breathless adoration in her voice. He'd never heard himself described that way by anyone. His conquests had been sporadic, and even then more animal than sensual. He'd given in to his needs only when he couldn't bear them any longer, and in his later years, it hadn't been that often. With Jennifer, it was different. He was touched by her headlong, helpless need of him. He'd thought that it was purely physical, but her eyes were telling him otherwise. A woman didn't look at a man like this when her only concern was fulfillment, and her shy blushing face made him uneasy.

He slid onto the bed beside her, turning her so that she was lying against him. He felt her flinch at the first touch of his aroused body, and he tilted her face so that he could see it.

"It's frightening for a woman with every new man, isn't it?" he asked absently. "Not knowing if he'll be gentle or cruel, demanding or brutal?"

"Yes. Of course," she lied. She could feel the heat of him, the threatening masculinity in a way she'd never dreamed of feeling it. She had to be careful. If she gave herself away, he'd never touch her. She wanted this with him so badly, refusing to admit even to herself that pregnancy was a very big part of the wanting, that her need of him included that faint possibility.

"I'm not cruel," he said, moving her so that she was completely against him. He felt the soft little tremors in her body as she stiffened in reaction before she relaxed and let him hold her closer. "I'm not brutal." He slid one lean hand along her side, over the curve of breast and waist and hip down to her smooth, soft thigh. He eased his leg between both of hers and brought her into intimacy. "And for your sake, I'll try not to be too demanding."

She gasped at the sudden stark contact.

"Shhhh," he whispered, smoothing the hair at her nape. "Lie still. It's better like this, lying on our sides. It's more intimate. Lift your leg over mine."

She blushed scarlet, praying that she wouldn't blow her cover. She did as he told her, but her hands were gripping his shoulders for dear life, biting in, and her stiffness was making him curious.

"Haven't you ever done it like this?" he whispered at her ear as his hands began to touch her intimately.

"No," she choked. It was true. But she'd never done it any way at all, including like this.

"Look at me."

She had to force her shocked, frightened eyes to meet his, and then she saw the curiosity narrowing them. He touched her where she was most a woman and she clenched her teeth to keep from crying out.

His firm lips parted as he probed delicately, holding her eyes. He scowled, because something was different here. Very different.

"Are you...are you going to use something," she managed, trying to divert him.

But it didn't work. He was experienced enough to recognize what was different, because this particular difference was so blatant that he didn't have to be a doctor to know what it was.

"My God," he whispered explosively. His hand stilled, but it didn't withdraw.

"Hunter..." she began, passion growing cold at the look on his face.

He searched her eyes and his hand moved. She bit her lip and tears threatened.

"Does this hurt, little one?" he whispered softly, and did it again. She tried not to flinch, but the intimacy and faint discomfort defeated her. "Yes," he answered his own question. His face mirrored his shock. He looked at her as if he'd never seen her before, and still that maddening hand didn't move away. He couldn't believe it. A woman with her beauty, at her age. A virgin.

"I didn't think you'd know," she stammered. "The books say that even a doctor can't tell..."

"That's true," he replied gently. "But you're intact, little one. Do you understand? Almost completely intact."

She swallowed, lowering her embarrassed eyes to the jerky rise and fall of his bronzed chest. "The doctors said that it would be uncomfortable, but that I wouldn't have to have surgery when the time came," she said finally. "It's mine to give," she added, lifting her face back to his.

"And you want to give it to me?" he asked gently.

"Yes."

He eased her over onto her back, his eyes soft and quiet and very dark. "Then give it to me this way, for now," he whispered. His mouth touched hers so tenderly that her heart ached, and his hand began to move very slowly, expertly, on her.

She tensed at the sudden shock of pleasure and tried to get away, but he threw a long, powerful leg across both of hers.

"No," he whispered into her mouth. "I'm going to take you up to the stars. Don't fight me," he said softly.

She trembled as the pleasure bit into her body. It came again, and again. And all the while he kissed her, his lips tender on her face while he made magic in her body. He saw the fear and smiled reassuringly, his voice coaxing, softly praising. He felt the urgency, felt when it reached breaking point. He knew exactly what to do, and when. Her back arched and she gasped, weeping as the pleasure took her, convulsing her under his delighted, fascinated gaze. Heat washed over him, blinding fire exploding, racking him even as he heard her cry out. Then, ages later, she relaxed, her tears hot and salty in his mouth as he kissed them away. He relaxed, too, because in the midst of her own explosive fulfillment, her movements had triggered his. He kissed her closed eyelids, thinking that never in his life had he experienced anything quite so perfect. And from such relatively innocent love play.

He lifted his head, turning hers toward him to search her drowned, shamed eyes.

"Is sex a sin for you?" he said softly. "Is that why you're a virgin?"

"There was never anyone I wanted enough," she whispered, sobbing. "I wanted you so badly. So much that I would have died to have you . . ."

He brushed her mouth with his, feeling humble. "Virginity is a rare gift," he whispered. "Yours to give, certainly. But not outside marriage. I have my own kind of honor, Jennifer. Taking your innocence without a commitment would violate everything I believe in." He lifted his lips from hers and searched her eyes quietly. "I won't take you. And, yes, I want to. I always have."

She swallowed the tears, wiping them away with the back of her hand. "I'm sorry if I hurt you," she said, avoiding his bold gaze.

"Hurt me how?"

She flushed.

He laughed gently. "Oh. That. No. I had as much pleasure from it as you did." He rolled over onto his back lazily and stretched, feeling years younger and full of life. He sprawled, aware of her fascinated eyes on his body, drinking in that feminine appreciation. "God, that was good," he said huskily. "Good! Like the first sip of water after the desert."

She sat up, a little self-conscious of her nudity, but his eyes were warm and admiring and she forgot her shyness. "But we didn't do anything, really," she said.

He brought her hand to his chest and caressed it. "I felt exactly what you did. The same need, the same sweet release." His head turned toward her. "Sleep with me."

She colored. "You just said..."

"That I wouldn't have sex with you," he agreed. "That isn't what I asked. Stay the night. We'll lie in each other's arms and sleep."

Her breath caught. "Could we?"

He drew her to his side, pillowing her head on his broad shoulder. "Yes. We could." His hand reached for the light, and he turned it out, folding her closer. "For tonight," he whispered at her ear, "we're lovers. Even if not conventional ones."

She closed her eyes with ecstasy, wanting to tell him everything, how she felt, how deeply she loved him, needed him. But she didn't dare. He thought it was just desire, and she had to let him keep thinking it. If he knew how involved she was emotionally, his pride wouldn't let him near her again. He wouldn't want to hurt her.

She flattened her hand on his chest and sighed. "This is heaven," she whispered.

He didn't echo the words back, but he could have. He'd never spent an entire night in a woman's arms. The need to keep Jennifer here kept him awake long after she relaxed in sleep.

The next morning, he kissed her awake. He was already dressed, but his eyes were enjoying the sight of her with the covers pulled away in a purely masculine way.

"Nymph," he murmured, sweeping a possessive hand down her body. "How can you be a virgin?"

"Pure living," she said, and laughed delightedly.

He brought her to her feet and kissed her softly. "You'd better get dressed. Morning is a bad time for men, and all my noble scruples aren't going to protect you if I have to look at you this way much longer."

She sighed and leaned against him. "There won't be a man," she whispered. "Not now."

His teeth ground together. Why in God's name did she have to say things like that? "Get dressed," he said tersely.

She was shocked at the sudden change in attitude, at his fierce anger. She pulled back from him, wounded, and searched for her clothes.

He didn't turn his back. He couldn't. He watched her dress, his heart pounding, his body aching for hers. It had taken all his willpower to drag himself out of bed this morning, when he wanted her to the point of madness. It had taken a cold shower and a self-lecture to get himself back in control.

"I wanted you last night," he said huskily. "I want you even more this morning. I'm not trying to be cruel, but the risk is just too damned great, do you understand?"

She was back in her gown now, everything under it in place. She nodded without really understanding and without looking at him and went to get her purse off the dresser, where he must have put it this morning. She took out a small brush and made some sense of her disheveled hair. She shouldn't feel like a fallen woman, she told herself. But she did. She'd thrown herself at him, and he hadn't wanted her enough to take the risk of involvement. It had been just a pleasant interlude to him. But to her, it had been everything.

He stood behind her, in dress slacks and shirt and tie and sports jacket, very urbane and sophisticated. His lean hands held her shoulders and he looked at their joint reflection, his eyes narrowing at the contrast.

"Dark and light," he said curtly. "Indian and white. If I gave you a baby, it would belong to both worlds and neither world. We could never have a child together."

So that was why he was so afraid of not being prepared with her. Because he didn't want her to have his child. It was so final . . .

She broke down and cried. He whipped her around and held her, rocking her, his arms fiercely possessive, the tremor in her body echoing in his.

"I could love you," he said roughly. "You could become the most important thing in my life. But I won't let it happen. We can't become involved. You have your world, I have mine." He tilted her mouth up to his and his dark eyes were frightening as they searched hers intently. "Kiss me. This is goodbye."

Her mouth opened for his, inviting it, giving him everything he asked for, everything he didn't. He groaned, lifting her into an intimate, exquisite embrace, and she whimpered because the pleasure was overwhelming. She clung to his powerful shoulders, breathing him, while the kiss reached its climax and left them both shaking. He let her slide to the floor, letting her feel his stark, urgent arousal. She was the cause of it; he was proud that he was such a man with her.

She took a slow breath, her mouth red from the aching kiss, and stepped back from him. Something died in her soft blue eyes as she looked up at him, but she managed a smile.

"Do you have a first name?" she whispered.

He nodded. "Phillip. I don't think I've ever told it to anyone else."

She fought back the tears. "Thank you." She turned away from him, picking up her purse with hands that shook. "I'd better go back to my room." She glanced back at him. "It was the best night of my life. I'll live on it forever."

She opened the door and ran out, blind and deaf, almost stumbling in her haste to get across the parlor of the suite to her own room. Such a short distance, yet it was like moving from one life to another, she thought, blind to the tormented face of the man she'd left behind.

Hunter watched her door close, and he leaned heavily against his door facing. It was for the best, he kept telling himself. But the memory of Jennifer in his arms was going to take years to fade. Maybe more years than he even had left.

Eight

Back in her own room, Jennifer changed from her evening dress into slacks and a short-sleeved red silk top, put her blond hair in a ponytail and tied it with a colorful red patterned scarf. But her heart wasn't in how she looked. Hunter had said goodbye, and what he meant was that they could work together for another ten years, but it would never again be more intimate than two colleagues.

She hoped that Eugene would be through with his politicking so that they could go home to Tulsa. She couldn't spend much more time around Hunter without going mad, especially after last night. He knew things about her now that no one else in the world did, and it was faintly unnerving.

His tenderness had surprised and delighted her, despite the circumstances. She wished she knew a little more about men. It occurred to her that a man who'd worked himself into a frenzy wanting a woman would have every right to be furious when he had to draw back. But Hunter hadn't been angry with her. He'd been kind. Did that mean that he hadn't wanted her very much in the first place, or did he care enough to put her feelings before his? She'd never been so confused, or so embarrassed. It was humiliating to have him know not only that she was on fire for him, but that she was a virgin to boot. If he wanted a weapon to use against her, he had a great one now. She dreaded facing him again. She had a feeling that last night wouldn't make any difference in his public treatment of her.

As it turned out, she was right. When she got downstairs to the restaurant for breakfast, Hunter stood, as did Eugene, for her to be seated, but his expression was stony and it gave away absolutely nothing.

"Good morning," Eugene said with a smile.

"You look very pretty," Cynthia added.

It wasn't a good morning, and Jennifer didn't feel pretty, she felt sick all over. She didn't quite meet Hunter's eyes as she sat down, mumbling something polite.

"Wasn't the ball wonderful?" Cynthia asked with a sigh. "I've never enjoyed anything quite as much."

"It was super," Jennifer said, staring blankly at her menu.

"I noticed that you were getting a lot of attention, Hunter," Eugene murmured dryly. "Especially from our host's sister."

"She wanted to see my scalps," he explained with a faint smile. He glanced toward Jennifer, his dark eyes giving nothing away. "Jennifer rescued me. We both had enough popularity to suit us by then, so we went back to the hotel."

"Sorry," Eugene said, sobering. "I hadn't realized I'd be putting you on the spot like that."

"I can handle social warfare," the younger man said imperturbably. "How did things work out?"

Eugene grinned. "Great. I got my deal. All we have to do is wait for the paperwork, and they're going to shoot that through. We should be able to send you two back down there to finalize the exact location within a month. I want to talk to two more people today. We'll fly home first thing in the morning."

At the mention of sending them back to the desert, Jennifer's face went paper white. Under the table, Hunter's lean hand caught hers where it lay on her lap. He enfolded it and his fingers contracted gently, sending a fiery thrill through Jennifer's body.

"I thought you knew where to look," Hunter replied.

Eugene nodded. "Oh, we do. What we're going to need you to do is camp out at a false location, to make sure our friends are led off the beaten track while we're running our seismic survey and doing flyovers."

"You don't think the agents will be able to hear dynamite blasts going off over the hill when our geologic technicians set up the seismic equipment to register the sound waves?" Jennifer asked with a smile. Hunter's strong fingers were warm and reassuring around her own, but they were making it hard to breathe normally.

"We'll work something out," Eugene said. He studied Jennifer's face with an intensity that made her nervous, especially when his calculating blue eyes went to Hunter. "Uh, you don't have any problem with spending a few more days out on the desert together?"

"Of course not," Hunter said easily.

"No," Jennifer agreed, and even smiled.

"You're both lying through your teeth." Eugene nodded slowly. "But I can't help it. You started this for me, you'll have to finish it. I'll try to work things so that we keep the field time to a minimum. Now. What shall we eat?''

Breakfast seemed to take forever. Jennifer still couldn't puzzle out Hunter's behavior. That lean hand wrapped around hers before breakfast had knocked half the breath out of her, even if his expression hadn't revealed anything.

While Eugene and Cynthia stood at the counter, Hunter caught Jennifer's arm and pulled her gently to one side.

"There's no need to look like that," he said softly, his dark eyes searching her shy ones. "It's all right."

"How do I look?" she asked.

"Embarrassed. Shamed." His hand dropped from her arm. "We did nothing last night that would have consequences. You understand?" he added, his dark eyes probing.

She turned red and swallowed hard. "Yes, I know," she said huskily. She couldn't meet his eyes.

"But it still embarrasses you to look at me?"

"Yes," she whispered.

His lean hand touched her long ponytail and he felt at a loss for words for the first time in recent memory. He didn't quite know what to say to her. She was nothing like the woman he'd thought her. He could hardly make himself believe that such a beautiful, desirable woman was totally innocent. And in so many ways. He looked at her mouth and felt again its soft, hungry response, felt the fierce need in her body that he'd wanted so desperately to satisfy. He still ached for her, but the shock of her chastity had spared him the shattering loss of honor he would have felt had he compromised her.

"You were a surprise, little one," he said half under his breath.

"And a big disappointment, I imagine, too," she replied.

"No." He gently tugged her ponytail until she looked up at him. "You don't have to worry about being alone with me on the desert. I'll take care of you. In every way."

She forced a smile. "I'll try not to be too much of a trial to you," she said quietly. "I'm...sorry...about what happened at the ball. I guess you know it all, now, don't you?"

"I know that you're vulnerable," he replied, his eyes soft and very dark. "I won't take advantage of it."

She searched his eyes with helpless attraction. "It's never been like that," she whispered worriedly. "Not ever..."

"We all have an Achilles' heel," he said. "Apparently I'm yours." He smiled gently. "It's all right. We'll muddle through."

"Do you have one?" she asked shyly.

"One what?"

"An Achilles' heel."

He chuckled softly. "Of course. Haven't you guessed yet what it is?"

"Your ancestry," she said with sudden insight.

"Smart lady." He noticed Eugene gesturing toward them and slid a careless arm around her shoulders. He couldn't help but feel the shiver that ran through her slender body, and he felt a little guilty at encouraging her physical infatuation for him. But it flattered his pride and touched his heart. If he didn't put some distance between them pretty soon, she could become a worse Achilles' heel even than his ancestry.

The day wore on, with Jennifer trying desperately not to look at Hunter with equal amounts of possession and wonder, and failing miserably. Eugene stayed in meetings until dinner, so Hunter escorted the women to all the places they hadn't seen before. Nothing had changed on the surface in Hunter's relationship with Jennifer. He didn't touch her except when it was necessary, and he didn't pay her any more attention than he paid Cynthia. Jennifer noticed that, and it made her feel even worse than she already did. The night before had been a revelation to her. But Hunter, even though he seemed a little less rigid with her, betrayed no sudden passion for her. By the time Eugene rejoined them and they had dinner at the restaurant that evening, Jennifer was more depressed than ever.

Hunter noticed her lack of spirit, and he was sorry. It had been equally difficult for him to pretend that nothing had happened. But for his sake as well as Jennifer's he had to keep things on a business basis from now on. He didn't dare risk a repeat of the night before. Having found Jennifer virginal had kept him awake all night. He wanted her more now than he ever had. It was agony to look at her and know that she'd give in to him with hardly any coaxing; to know that she'd give him what she'd never given another man.

He watched her all through dinner, hungry to get her alone, to kiss her until she was too weak to stand up. He didn't dare, of course. He was going to have to think of something to keep him occupied tonight and out of trouble.

Fate did it for him. He went with the women upstairs while Eugene had a drink with another contact. He'd suggested that they go by their suite first, to drop off Jennifer, trying not to notice the wounded look on her young face. But just as they rounded the corner off the elevator, they spotted a man coming out of Jennifer's room.

"Stay here," he said tersely, jerking out his .45 automatic. He was off in one single graceful movement.

Jennifer wanted to scream after him to be careful, her heart in her eyes, her pulses jerking wildly as he pursued the other man down the corridor and around another corner.

"Oh, Lord," Cynthia said huskily, putting a protective arm around Jenny.

"He was in my room," Jennifer said. "I hope he doesn't hurt Hunter! It's got to be some of that same group who broke into my apartment before. They're after my maps!"

"But you didn't bring them, did you?" Cynthia asked worriedly.

"Hunter has them," Jennifer said huskily. "But he hides things well. I suppose my room was the natural one to search."

"Risky for them to come here," Cynthia commented.

Jenny's thoughts were occupied with the man chasing the prowlers. She didn't hear the other woman's words. "I wish Hunter would come back!" She stared down the corridor worriedly.

He did, a minute later, pushing his automatic back into its holster on the way. He looked and felt furiously angry. Just the thought that the agent could have broken into Jenny's room while she was in it, asleep, made him crazy.

"He got out on a fire escape. There was a car waiting, damn the luck," Hunter said angrily. "We'll have to arrange something for tonight."

"Jennifer can stay with me, and you can stay with Eugene," Cynthia volunteered.

"No." Hunter didn't look at Jennifer. "You're safer with Eugene. I'll be in the suite with Jennifer. Nobody will get in."

"You could sleep on the sofa," Jennifer volunteered with downcast eyes, thrilled that he was being so protective.

"We'll discuss it after we leave Cynthia at her door. I'll post an operative outside it tonight. You'll be safe until Eugene comes up," he promised Cynthia.

"You're very efficient," Cynthia said with a smile, and a teasing glance at Jennifer.

Jennifer didn't say a word. She went along to drop Cynthia off and then minutes later she was alone with Hunter in her room. He had some odd instrument and he went over the entire apartment with it, careful to check everywhere. He discovered two tiny metal devices, which he dealt with before he said a word.

"I've sent a man down to my room to play possum," he told her, shucking his jacket. The shoulder holster was firm around his broad chest, the dark butt of the handle stark against his white shirt.

She shivered at the sinister outline of the gun, at the memory of how Hunter earned his living. Sometimes she could forget it altogether, but not at times like this, and she feared for him.

He saw that nervous scrutiny and lifted an eyebrow. "I won't shoot you by mistake," he murmured dryly.

"It's not that." She wrapped her arms around his chest. "They never give up, do they?"

"From what you've told me about strategic metals, I'm not surprised." He moved closer, his lean hands smoothing over her shoulders. "Lie down and get some sleep, if you can. In the morning we'll go home. A couple of weeks in the desert while things are finalized, and we'll be home free. No more danger."

"Yes." And no more interludes like this. She thought it, but she didn't say it.

His dark eyes held hers. "Go on," he said gently. "I told you last night, there won't be any more close calls."

"I know. I'm a little nervous about the intruder, that's all," she lied.

"Of course." He knew she was lying. He watched her put away the clothes that had been disarranged, seeing the way she grimaced at the thought of strange hands on her things. But she packed them before she got out a night-gown. He was standing in the doorway, and his expression was grim.

"Are you . . . going to stay there while I change?" she asked huskily.

His jaw tautened. "If I did, you wouldn't spend the night alone."

He turned away and closed the door, trying not to picture Jennifer's soft, nude body in that room.

It was a long night, but there were no incidents. The next morning when Jennifer got up and dressed, Hunter was on his way out of the suite.

"Marlowe's outside the door," he said tersely. "We leave for the airport in thirty minutes."

"I'll be ready," she said quietly.

He nodded curtly and closed the door behind him.

They flew back to Tulsa that morning, but Jennifer barely had time to get settled back in her apartment before she and Hunter were on a plane heading to southern Arizona all over again.

"Same song, second verse," she murmured as they took the camping equipment back out to the desert, having gone through the process of renting a four-wheel-drive vehicle and buying camping equipment all over again.

He glanced at her, a smoking cigarette in his hand. "Well, it's not quite so bad. This time you don't have to do any real prospecting. We're only camping out."

"No television, no movies. Just the two of us and a handful of enemy agents, right?" she mused, trying not to give away how miserable she was.

"It won't be that bad," he said with a faint smile. "I'll teach you how to track and all about Apache customs. We'll get by."

She nodded. "With bullets whizzing around us and people trying to kill us for a mineral strike, right?"

"Stop that. Nobody's going to try to kill you. They want the land, not bodies."

She wished that was reassuring, but it wasn't.

They pitched the tent at the site they'd occupied the first night when they were here before. It was a good six miles from the actual site, but still close enough that seismic tests could be detected with the right monitors. But Eugene was an old fox, and her rock samples had been assayed by now. He used seismic tests extensively when he was searching for oil deposits, but moly was a different element and there were all sorts of detecting devices he could use to search out deposits.

"Nervous?" Hunter asked as they pitched camp.

She nodded. "A little."

He built a fire and proceeded to prepare food, a process Jennifer watched with fascination.

"Hunter, did you grow up around here?" he asked suddenly.

He nodded. "I used to wander all over this country as a boy. Within limits, of course. I kept to the reservation."

She studied him across the camp fire. "And now?"

He looked up, studying her face in the flames. Even in jeans and a floppy T-shirt she was gorgeous, he thought. "Now I live in Tulsa."

"You said you kept horses."

"Yes. On the reservation. I own a small homestead. The house is my refuge. Actually I should say that the tribe owns the land, and ownership is overseen by the tribal council. We aren't allowed to sell any land without approval from the Bureau of Indian Affairs. The reasoning for that is a long story, and one I'd rather not go into right now," he added when she started to speak.

"All right," she said easily. He handed her a plate of stew and a cup of black coffee, adding a couple of slices of loaf bread to her plate. She ate hungrily. "Something about the night air gives me an appetite," she sighed when she finished. "Look at the stars. They're bigger here. And it's so quiet . . . Well, except for the coyotes and an occasional four-wheel-drive vehicle and the sound of rifle fire as people shoot road signs for amusement."

He glanced at her ruefully. "You're poetic."

"Oh, very." She wrapped her hands around her knees and stared at them.

He watched her for a minute, remembering another night alone, at another camp site, and her bare breasts in the moonlight. He got up suddenly.

"I'll have a look around. You might go ahead and turn in. It's been a long day."

"Yes, I think I will," she agreed easily. She went into the tent and got into her sleeping bag. Amazingly she was asleep when he finally came to bed.

The days went by all too slowly, and by the end of the week, Jennifer's nerves were raw and she was snapping at

Hunter. He wasn't in any too good a humor himself. Jennifer lying beside him in the tent night after night was driving him out of his mind. The scent of her, the sound of her, the sight of her were so firmly imbedded in his brain that he felt part of her already.

The memories didn't help. He'd come so close to possessing her, and now his body knew the reality of hers and wanted it. The hunger kept gnawing at him, making him impatient and irritable.

"Must you keep turning those scanners on?" Jennifer asked when the police scanner began to get on her nerves the Friday night after they'd arrived.

"Yes, I must," he said tersely. "They're reporting an incident near here—presumably at the test site where Eugene's geologic technicians are working. I'm going to have a look. Stay close to the tent. Have you still got that .22 rifle I gave you?"

"Yes, and I can use it," she replied. "Was anybody hurt?" she asked.

"If I knew that, why would I be going to check it out?" he asked curtly. "What a damned stupid question!"

"Well, I'm not a trained agent, so you'll have to forgive my ignorance!" she shot back. "Go ahead and get shot! I won't cry over you!"

"I never expected that you would," he returned. He got into the four-wheel drive and took off without looking back.

Jennifer's nerve deserted her the minute the Jeep disappeared. She sat down beside the scanner and listened to it uneasily, glancing around with the rifle across her legs. She didn't know what had happened, and the fact that the agents were the most likely people to be bothering the technicians was unsettling news. What if they came here and tried to shake the information they wanted out of her while Hunter was gone?

That was ridiculous, of course. She laughed out loud. Of course they wouldn't come here . . .

The sound of a Jeep alerted her and she jumped up. Hunter, she thought with relief. She ran toward the rutted road with the rifle in time to be caught in the headlights of the vehicle that was approaching. There was an exclamation and a shot as the vehicle suddenly reversed and rushed off in the other direction.

Jennifer felt something hot against her arm, like a sudden sting. She touched it and her fingers came away wet.

She looked down at her arm. She could see a dark stain in the faint light from the camp fire. She lifted her fingers closer and the unmistakable smell of blood was on her hand!

I've been shot, she thought in astonishment. My God, I've been shot!

She sat down heavily next to the camp fire, with the rifle still in her shaking hands. If only Hunter would come back! She was alone and afraid and she didn't know what to do. Obviously the agents had come roaring into camp with the intention of seeking information. They hadn't expected her to come running toward them with a rifle. They'd shot at her in apparent self-defense and had raced away before she could get a shot off at them. It might be funny later. Right now, it was terrifying.

Her arm hurt. She grimaced. The sound of a vehicle approaching came again, but this time, she didn't run toward it. She raised the rifle, wincing as her arm protested, and leveled it at the dark shape spurting into camp.

"That's far enough!" she called out.

The engine and lights were cut off. The door opened. "Shoot and be damned," Hunter's deep voice replied.

Nine

Jenny thought that as long as she lived, she'd never forget the expression on Hunter's face when she collapsed in his arms and he discovered that she'd been shot.

She managed to explain what had happened while he laid her gently on her sleeping bag inside the tent and moved the Coleman lantern closer to check the wound.

"I must have passed them coming back. Damn it!" he burst out, adding something in a very gutteral language that seemed to raise and lower in pitch and stop suddenly between syllables.

"Is that...cursing?" she asked.

"Yes, and thank your stars you can't translate it," he added icily. He glanced down at her. "They raided the other camp, but they were a little too late. The technicians flew back to Tulsa this afternoon with the data. They left the tents and other gear, just as Eugene had instructed, to give them time to get away. They were supposed to contact us, but apparently they were being watched too closely.''

"Eugene will kill them," she murmured, groaning when his fingers touched around the gash in her soft skin.

"If he doesn't, I will," he returned. "Which is nothing to what I intend doing to the man who shot you."

She stared up at him through waves of pain. His eyes were frightening, and at that moment he looked pagan, untamed.

"It isn't bad," she said, trying to ease the tension she could almost taste as his hard, deft fingers searched around the cut. They seemed just slightly unsteady. Imagine anything shaking the stoic Mr. Hunter, she thought with hysterical amusement.

"I can't see properly in this light. Come on." He helped her to the vehicle and helped her into the passenger side. He turned on the overhead light after he'd climbed quickly in beside her, and once more his eyes were on the cut. "You can manage without stitches, but it needs an antiseptic."

"There might be a drugstore..." she offered.

He turned off the light and started the engine. He never seemed to feel the need to answer questions, she sighed to herself. Amazing how he expected her to read his mind.

"But what about our things?" she asked.

He cursed again, turning around. "Wait here." He left the engine running, put out the camp fire, got her case and his out of the tent along with the technical gear, and left the rest of it.

"But the tent, the sleeping bags..." she began. He glanced at her and she stopped when she saw his expression. She cleared her throat. "Never mind."

He set off into the desert and drove for what seemed forever until he came to a small house, set against the jagged peak of one of southern Arizona's endless mountain chains. He pulled into the dirt driveway, and Jenny wondered whose home it was. The house was livable, just, but it needed painting and patching and a new roof.

"Come on." He opened the door and helped her out.

"It's a beautiful setting," she murmured as she drank in the sweet, clear air and looked around the yard at the ocotillo and cholla and agave that surrounded the yard. "Like being alone in the world."

"I've always thought so," he said stiffly. He escorted her onto the porch and produced a key to unlock the door. He didn't look at her as he opened it and pulled the screen door back to let her enter the living room.

It was nothing like the exterior of the house, she noticed as he pulled a long chain and the bare light bulb in the ceiling came on. The living room was comfortable and neat, with padded armchairs and cane-bottomed chairs, Indian rugs on the floors and spread over the backs of the chairs. There was some kind of furry round shield with tiny fur tails hanging from it, and basketry everywhere.

Hunter was watching her, waiting for disgust or contempt to show on her soft face. But she seemed fascinated; almost charmed by what she saw.

She turned back to him, her eyes shining despite the faint throb of the wound on her arm. "It's your house, isn't it?" she asked.

His dark eyebrows arched. "Yes."

"You're wondering how I knew," she murmured dryly. "It's simple. You're the only person I know who would enjoy living totally alone in the world with no nosy neighbors. And this," she gestured toward the living room, "is how I'd picture your living room."

He managed a faint smile. "Come on. I'll put a patch on the injury, then I'll find something to cook."

"All right."

"No comment about the cooking?" he added, leading her into a stark white bathroom with aging fixtures.

"I'd be surprised if you couldn't cook. You seem so self-sufficient."

"I've always had to be," he said simply. He stripped off his jacket, rolled up his sleeves and got out medicine and bandages from the cabinet over the sink. "My father died when I was small. I lived with my grandfather, on the reservation, until I was old enough to enlist. When I got out of the Green Berets, I kicked around for a few years doing other things. Eventually Ritter offered me a job and I've been there ever since."

"No wife, ever?" she asked hesitantly.

His dark, quiet eyes met hers. "Women don't fit in a place like this," he said. "It's stark and bare-bone comfort, and it's lonely. In case you haven't guessed, this is part of the reservation, too." He waited for her reaction, but there wasn't one. He shrugged and continued. "I'm away most of the time. I've never asked anyone to share it because I don't think a woman could. My job would be an immediate point of contention and my heritage would be another. I live on the reservation," he added with a mocking smile. "I can see how that would go over with most in-laws. And I believe in some of the old ways, especially in family life."

"A woman's place is three steps behind the man..." she began.

"A man should behave as one," he returned simply. "And a woman has her place—a very special place—in the order of things. She gives life, nurtures it. She gives warmth and light to her man, her children." He ran a basin of water, found a cloth and bathed the wound on Jenny's arm. "But, no, I don't think her place is three steps behind her man, or that she becomes property when she marries. Perhaps you don't know, but in the old days, many Apache women fought right alongside their men and were as respected as the warriors."

"No, I didn't know," she confessed. The touch of his fingers was painful delight. Her eyes glanced over the hard lines of his dark face with pure pleasure. "You're proud of your ancestry, aren't you?"

He looked down at her. "My people are like a separate state, under federal jurisdiction," he replied. "We have our own laws, our own reservation police, our own code of behavior. When we live in your world, we seem alien." He laughed coldly. "I wish I could tell you how many times in my life I've been called Tonto or Chief, and how many fights I've been into because of it."

She was beginning to understand him. He'd grown a shell, she supposed, because of the difficulties. And now he was trapped in it and couldn't find his way out.

"I know a little about prejudice," she said, surprising him. "I'm a female geologist and I work in the oil business." She smiled. "Equality is all the rage in accounting and law firms back east, and even in corporations. But out in the boondocks in the oil exploration game, there are Neanderthal men who think a woman goes to those lonely places for just one reason. I wish I had a nickel for every time I've had to threaten someone with a suit for sexual harassment."

"Looking the way you do, I can understand your problem," he mused, glancing at her with dancing dark eyes. "How does this feel?" he added when he'd put antiseptic on the wound and lightly bandaged it.

"It feels much better, thank you," she said. Her eyes searched his dark face while he put away the medicine. "What do you mean, the way I look?"

He closed the cabinet and gazed down at her. His face was expressionless except for the dark, disturbing glitter in his eyes as they slid down her body and up again. "Is it important to hear me say it?" he asked. "You know how lovely you are."

Her breath caught. "I've been told I was," she corrected. "It never meant anything. Before."

His jaw clenched. He stared at her until she flushed and still his eyes didn't waver or even blink. "Be careful," he said quietly. "I still want you very badly."

"I'm twenty-seven years old," she whispered. "If it isn't you, it won't be anybody. Ever. I said that once. I meant it."

His breath expelled roughly. He caught her around the waist and pulled her up from the edge of the bathtub where she'd been sitting. His arm was steely strong, and the feel and scent of him so close made her almost moan with pleasure.

"How much do you know about birth control?" he asked bluntly.

"I know that babies come if you don't use any," she replied, trying to sound sophisticated with a beet-red face.

His eyes were relentless. "And do you think I'm prepared for casual interludes with women all the time?"

"Most men are," she faltered.

"I'm not most men," he returned. "These days I think of sex as something that goes hand in hand with love, respect, honor. It used to be a casual amusement when I was a young man. I'm thirty-seven now, and it isn't casual or amusing anymore. It's serious business."

She could have reminded him that for a few minutes one night, he'd forgotten all those reasons, but she didn't. Her eyes fell to his firm chin. "It isn't casual with me, either," she whispered "But I'd give anything...!" She bit her lip. "I'm sorry."

His hand came up, framing her own chin, lifting her eyes to his. "You'd give anything...?" he prompted slowly.

She closed her eyes so that he wouldn't see the longing. So that she wouldn't throw herself at him again, as she had that night in Washington. "Nothing. I'm just tired. I wasn't thinking."

"I know you're infatuated with me," he said out of the blue.

Her eyes flew open, startled. "What?"

"It isn't something you hide well," he replied. His eyes narrowed. "I've had hell trying not to take advantage of it. I'm a new experience for you, something out of the ordinary, and I know already how you seek the unusual. But since you don't know, I'll tell you. Sex is the same with an Apache as it is with a white man, in case you—"

He broke off because she slapped him, with the full strength of her arm behind the blow. Tears welled in her eyes; her face had gone white with shock and grief.

He didn't flinch. He let her go, very gently, and moved away. "I'll see about something to eat," he said, with no inflection at all in his voice as he started toward the kitchen.

Jenny cried. She closed the bathroom door and cried until her throat hurt. If he'd tried for months to think up something hurtful, he couldn't have succeeded any better. She knew he was aware of her desire for him, but she hadn't known he was aware of her feelings, too. It made her too vulnerable.

Finally she dried her eyes and went out without looking in the small mirror. She could imagine what she looked like without having to see herself.

He glanced at her and his expression hardened as he proceeded to fry steak and eggs. "I'd expected to spend the weekend here, so I loaded up on supplies yesterday," he said. "You can set the table."

She took the dishes from the cabinet he gestured toward and set two places, including a mug for the coffee that was brewing in the modern coffeepot. She took her time meticulously folding two paper towels to go at each place.

"Utensils?" she asked in a totally defeated tone.

"Here." He opened the drawer beside him, but as she moved closer to reach inside it, he turned suddenly and pulled her to him. His mouth eased down over hers with a gentle, insistent pressure that caught her completely off guard. She felt his strong teeth nipping tenderly at her lower lip until her mouth opened for him. Then she felt his tongue inside, touching her own, his arm contracting, the sound that echoed out of his throat, deep and gruff and faintly threatening.

Her nails bit into his back where her arms had gone under his and around him, and she bit off a short, sharp little cry as the pleasure cut the ground from under her feet. The injury to her arm was still throbbing, but she held on for dear life, uncaring in the thrall of such aching pleasure. She didn't want him to stop, not ever!

All too soon, he lifted his head. His eyes were dark with emotion, his jaw clenched. "Finish setting the table," he said huskily, and abruptly let her go to concentrate on the Spanish omelet he was making.

She couldn't help the trembling of her hands as she complied with that request. It wasn't until they were halfway through the impromptu meal and the strong, fresh coffee that she was able to get some kind of control over herself.

"To continue what I started to say when we were in the bathroom, I'm not prepared for an intimate encounter," he said when she laid down her fork. He didn't look at her as he said it. His eyes were on the coffee cup in his hand. "And as I told you in Washington that night, half-breed children belong in no one's world."

Her eyes searched his face. A suspicion at the back of her mind began to take shape. He looked Apache. There was no doubt about that part of his heritage. But the way he felt about mixing the races, wasn't it violent if he'd never had experience of it?

"Which one of your parents was white, Phillip?" she asked softly.

His head jerked up. His eyes flashed at her. "What did you say?" he asked in a tone that should have backed her down. It didn't.

"I said, which one of your parents was white?"

"I'd forgotten that I told you my given name," he said softly. "You've never used it."

She began to realize, belatedly, that it was her use of his first name that had rattled him, not her reference to his parentage. She hesitated. "I didn't realize I had," she said after a minute.

He leaned back, troubled, the coffee cup still in his lean, dark hand. He watched her intently. "My mother was white, Jennifer," he said finally.

"Is she still alive?"

He shrugged. "I don't know. She couldn't take life on the reservation, and my father was too Apache to leave it. She left when I was five and I haven't seen her since. My father died a year later. He gave up. Life without her, he said, was no life. I always consider that I lost both my parents when I was five, so I don't qualify the statement. I don't know where my mother is." His face hardened. "I don't care. Her family put me through school and supported me while I was younger. I didn't find out until I was much older. My grandfather never would have told me, but I found a check stub. He was a proud man." He looked down at his hands. "Life on the reservation is hard. Unemployment, infant mortality, poverty... It's no one's idea of the American dream. He took the money for my sake, not for his. What he didn't spend on me, he sent back."

She stretched her hand toward his free one, lying on the table and abruptly stopped. He wouldn't want sympathy, she supposed.

But surprisingly, his own hand slid the remaining distance and enveloped hers, his thumb softly stroking her palm. "White and brown," he observed, staring at the differences in color. "I'm still Apache, Jenny, despite my white blood. But if I had a child with a white woman, he'd be a lost soul, like me. Caught between two worlds. My own people have a hard time accepting me, even though I look more Apache than white."

Her eyes adored him. "I can't imagine a more handsome man of either race," she said quietly.

His face went a ruddy color, and she wondered if it was possible to embarrass him.

She smiled wickedly. "My, my, are you *blushing*?"

He let go of her hand with an outright laugh. "Compliments are difficult for me," he said gruffly. "Eat your omelet."

She picked up her fork with a sigh, wincing a little as the movement made her arm uncomfortable. "Can I ask why we aren't having bacon or sausage with our eggs?" she murmured.

"Apaches don't eat pork," he said. "Or fish. Ever."

"Why?" she asked, astonished.

"Beats me. We just don't."

"I thought I knew something about your people. I suppose I don't know much at all."

He smiled to himself. "You know more than most whites."

"I guess that operative of yours who's Papago knows more," she murmured without looking at him. "She's the kind of woman you'll marry one day, isn't she?"

He frowned down at his omelet. "I don't know that I'll marry at all," he said. He lifted his eyes to her sad face and felt a wave of grief that almost knocked him flat. She was infatuated with him, but she could never endure life here. She was beautiful and sweet and he wanted her until she was all but an obsession. But his mind kept insisting that he couldn't risk having her turn out like his mother. His mother hadn't been able to take living in an Indian world.

She sighed wearily. "I've had the same feeling lately. I'm almost twenty-eight. Despite the fact that women are becoming mothers later and later in life, I don't really like the risk factors after thirty-five." She smiled at her omelet as she cut it. "Funny. I always thought I might make a pretty good mother."

"You've had the opportunity to marry," he said stiffly.

"Oh, of course. Soft, carefree city men who have affairs and look upon marriage as slow death. I had one proposal from a man who was twenty years older than me and wanted to live in Alaska." She glanced up. "I hate polar bears."

He smiled. "So do I."

"My other proposal was from a boy my age when I was eighteen, and he only wanted to marry me to get away from his parents. He was rich and I wasn't—it was a sort of rebellion." She put down her fork. "I've never been asked to marry anybody because I was loved. Wanted, yes. But that wasn't enough.''

"You're not over the hill," he reminded her.

"It doesn't matter." She looked up at him, her eyes wide and soft and gentle. "I'm sorry you stopped that night in Washington," she said huskily. "I wouldn't have regretted it, ever."

His jaw tautened. He finished his steak and washed it down with coffee. "It would have hurt like hell."

She traced the rim of her plate, her heart beating madly at the memory of his arms around her, his body intimately over her own. "It wouldn't have hurt long," she whispered. "I wanted you too badly to care."

"God, yes, you did," he said through his teeth. The memories were driving him crazy. "Shaking in my arms, and I'd barely touched you. By the time I put my mouth on yours, you were trembling all over with the need. I never dreamed that women felt it like that."

"Maybe most women don't feel it like that," she said uneasily. "Maybe there's, well, something wrong with me...."

"There's nothing wrong with you that a night in my arms wouldn't cure," he said curtly. His dark eyes caught her blue ones and held them hotly. "But it would only be a night, and we'd have the rest of our lives to regret it."

Her lips parted as she searched his eyes. "No, we wouldn't," she whispered. "And you know it. You want me just as much as I want you."

He nodded slowly, his gaze dropping to her full breasts and back up again to her mouth and her eyes. "You can only give your chastity once."

"I know that, too," she replied. "I meant what I said. If it isn't you, it won't be anybody." Her breath sighed out raggedly. "I love you," she said achingly.

He let out a long, weary sigh. After a minute he got up and held out his hand. She took it, feeling his lean fingers enfold hers, wrap gently around them.

He led her into his bedroom without speaking and closed the door. "Do you want the light out?" he asked.

She bit her lower lip. She wanted to be sophisticated and worldly, but she was already blushing.

He smiled with bitter irony. "Never mind." He reached up and turned off the light, leaving the room in almost total darkness, except for the half moon that left its yellow shadow over the patchwork quilt on the bed.

"What do we do now?" she whispered, her voice husky with excitement and faint apprehension.

"What we did in my hotel room that night in Washington," he murmured as his hands reached for her. "Except that this time I won't pull back when I feel the barrier..."

"Phillip." She moaned his name into his mouth as it came down on hers, gasping when she felt him pull her hips roughly into the already aroused thrust of his.

"This is how badly I want you," he whispered, his breathing mingling with hers. "It happens the minute your body touches mine. Magic."

"Yes." She pulled his shirt out of his jeans and slid her hands up against his bare back, feeling the taut muscles, the rough silk of his skin. It was cool, and seconds later when her bare breasts melted into the hard wall of his chest, that was cool, too, against the heated warmth of her own skin.

When he had every scrap of material away from their bodies, he lifted her, with his mouth gently moving on her own, and laid her on the quilt. His hand went to the bedside table. He opened a drawer and removed something. Seconds later, he placed it in her hand and taught her how to put it in place. Even that was exciting and sensual in the hot darkness.

"This is so we won't make a baby," he whispered, his voice deep and slow as he moved over her. His teeth nibbled softly at her upper lip. His lean hands smoothed down her body, lingering on her soft thighs, making her tremble with the pleasure of his touch.

Her body was shivering. He kissed her tenderly, and then his mouth moved down to her breasts and caressed their hard tips until she was writhing under him.

"You like that, don't you?" he whispered. "I like it, too, little one. You taste of satin here, and of desire here," he breathed against a taut nipple, his lips pulling at it with sensual tenderness.

She clung to his muscular arms, her breath coming in jerks while he kissed and touched and tasted, the darkness like a warm blanket over her fears.

When she was shuddering, he eased her trembling legs apart and levered himself down between them, his mouth poised just above her own, his eyes glittered into hers in the darkness. He probed tenderly and felt her tense.

"When I push down, try not to do that," he whispered. "If you tense up, it's going to hurt more."

She shivered with delicious anticipation, her body throbbing with a heat it had never felt before. Her legs moved to admit him even closer and her nails bit into his shoulders. "I'll try," she breathed.

His chest rose and fell deeply. His hips moved down, and she made a noise deep in her throat as she felt the burning pain. She tensed involuntarily. "I'm . . . sorry," she gasped.

"It can't be be helped," he said quietly. "I'm going to have to hurt you. Cry out if you want to. I'm sorry . . . !"

She did, because it was worse than she'd imagined it would be. But she didn't fight him or try to push him away even then. She bit her lip and moaned, trying to force her body to relax as it protested the invasion of his.

"Only a little longer," he whispered. His mouth came closer. "Kiss me. It will help."

She let him take her mouth, opened it to admit the slow, deep penetration of his tongue that imitated what his body was doing to hers. It was so erotic that it tricked her taut muscles into relaxing, and suddenly what had been almost impossible was easy and smooth.

He heard her intake of breath and lifted his head, smiling down at her through his own fierce excitement. The act of possession was almost enough to trigger his fulfillment. He had to stop and breathe himself to keep control.

"Phillip," she whispered achingly. Her eyes sought his, and she could barely believe it was happening, at last.

"How does it feel?" he whispered at her lips.

"Incredible," she managed, her voice shaking.

"And we haven't begun," he breathed as his mouth began to open on hers. His hips lifted and moved and she shivered, because the surge of pleasure she felt shocked her.

The sound of the car roaring up outside was an interruption that froze them both in incredulous shock.

"My God," he ground out. "No!"

But the car was stopping. Worse, there were lights flashing, so it had to be a police car.

He lifted himself away from her, shuddering as he fell onto his back and arched. He groaned and stiffened, while Jennifer tried to weather the frustration and anger she felt.

There were footsteps on the porch and a loud, heavy knock at the door.

"Just a minute!" Hunter shouted. He got up, pulling on his jeans with hands that shook. "God almighty, I'll kill someone for this!" he muttered. He leaned over Jennifer's shivering body and bent to kiss her with rough hunger. "Get dressed, quickly."

He left the room and she turned on the light, hurrying to get back into her clothes and make some kind of order in the room. She brushed her hair with his hairbrush and, satisfied that she looked as presentable as possible, she opened the bedroom door.

Hunter was talking to another man. They had to be speaking Apache, because Jennifer couldn't understand a word.

"This is Choya," Hunter introduced the shorter man. "He's chief of the reservation police. I've been telling him what happened. Since the incident occurred on Apache land, he'll be responsible for the investigation and any arrests."

"In other words, I get all the headaches," the newcomer grinned, perfect white teeth flashing. "My God, Hunter, I go home to a wife with buck teeth and you have her." He shook his head. "I need to change medicine men."

Hunter chuckled. "You know Maria's the prettiest woman around, so shut up. Is there anything else you need to know?"

"Not tonight," Choya said, and exchanged a knowing glance with Hunter. "Sorry about my timing. I'll get back on the road now. Good night."

"Good night," Jennifer said, blushing all over.

Hunter closed the door behind him and turned to Jennifer. He didn't move until the car drove away, his dark

eyes sliding over her, his dark, bare chest lifting and falling slowly.

"Come here," he said curtly.

She went to him without hesitation. He lifted her, but
instead of carrying her back into the bedroom, he carried
her to the rocking chair and sat down with her across his
lap.

"Thanks to Choya, we can't finish what we started," he
said, smiling into her heated face. "I was prepared, but
only for one time." He bent and drew his mouth slowly
over hers. "Still burning?" he breathed.

His hand was on the buttons of her blouse, which she
put on without her bra, and now he knew it. She arched,
letting him look, letting him touch.

Her fingers tangled in his dark hair and pulled, tugging his face toward her bare breasts.

"All right," he whispered. "Is this what you want?"

It was. Oh, it was, she thought in sweet anguish, loving the touch of his mouth on her velvety skin. She lay in
his arms and made no protest when he stripped off her
jeans and underwear. His hand found her and moved, and
his mouth reached up for hers. He rocked the chair and
touched her rhythmically, and the combined force of the
sensual movements very quickly brought an explosive
culmination in her taut body.

She cried out and shivered and was still. He gathered
her close beside him, her breasts brushing his bare chest,
his cheek against her hair.

"It isn't enough," he whispered. "But it's safe. One
day, so help me, I'll put you under me in bed and fill you
until you scream."

She bit his shoulder in anguished need, and he shuddered and brought her even closer. "What about you?"
she asked huskily.

"Don't worry about me," he said, ignoring his own need. He could handle it. He'd have to, he couldn't take the risk.

"You're no longer a virgin, technically," he said, lifting his head to search her eyes. "Despite the fact that we were barely together, I had your virginity tonight."

She smiled up at him with awe. "Yes."

He touched her mouth, tracing her lips with a finger that wasn't quite steady. "And you don't regret it?"

"No," she whispered.

His jaw clenched as his eyes fell to her bare breasts. "Neither do I," he said. "You belong to me."

"I know."

His eyes flashed as they met hers. "There won't be another man."

"I know that, too."

He stared into her eyes for a long moment, then he stood and carried her back into the bedroom. He stripped himself before he turned out the light and put her under the covers. He drew her body against his and pressed her cheek into his bare shoulder with a long, rough sigh.

"In the morning, get up as quickly as you can," he said at her ear. "A man awakens aroused and his wits are dulled by it. Don't be tempted to take chances. I won't forget and I won't forgive."

She sighed. "All right," she said reluctantly. She closed her eyes, pressing her hand flat on his chest and curling into his taut body. "Good night, Phillip."

His hand covered hers. "Good night, little one." He brushed a careless kiss against her forehead and then her eyes, lingering on the thick, long lashes.

"I'm sorry," she whispered.

"For what?"

"You had nothing."

His body was taut but he tried to ignore it. "I'll live," he murmured, trying to keep his voice light.

But she heard the stress in it. Hesitantly she slid her hand down his body and felt him tense. She waited for him to stop her, but he didn't. She heard his breathing change and felt his body arch in a slow, delicate rhythm. Her fingers moved down and he arched into them.

"Yes," he whispered, his eyes closed.

She stroked him, feeling him throb, feeling him tauten, hearing the anguished groan that broke from his lips as her hand explored him.

"Do it," he bit off.

He taught her, kicking the covers off, his eyes glittering in the darkness. She heard his breathing become tortured, watched his body react to her shy, loving touch. He watched her until it became impossible and then he arched up, crying out, and she learned things about men that all her reading hadn't prepared her for.

Eventually they slept. She supposed that she should regret what had happened. If she ever did marry, even if she hadn't been totally seduced, she was no longer completely chaste. But it was Hunter she'd given that privilege to, and she had no regrets. She loved him so deeply that she could live on tonight, forever if she had to.

She got up the next morning and went into the living room with shy reluctance. She never quite knew what to expect from Hunter, because he was so unpredictable.

He was putting food on the table. He glanced up. "I was about to call you," he said politely. "Sit down."

It was as if nothing had ever happened between them. She stared at him curiously as she sat in the chair.

He poured coffee with a straight face. "How's the arm?"

"It's sore, but I think it will be all right."

"We'll get you to a doctor before we leave for the airport. We're going home today."

"So soon?"

"It's past time," he returned tersely, and the eyes that met hers were angry. "Last night should never have happened. You have a very disturbing effect on my willpower, and I'm tired of it. I'm taking you back to Tulsa. If there's another assignment like this, I'll send one of my operatives with you instead. There aren't going to be any repeats."

She lowered her eyes to the table. "You can't bear to lose control in any way, can you?"

"No," he replied honestly. "You're becoming a liability, and I can't afford one. My job requires total concentration. What I feel when I'm around you could get us both killed. I made a mistake last night that could have been fatal. I left you alone. If we hadn't been at each other's throats out of simple physical frustration, I'd have had the presence of mind to take you with me. But I didn't."

"I'm all right," she said quietly.

"You could have died. Or I could have. I've had enough emotional stress to last me a lifetime, Jennifer," he said, his voice final. "From now on, I'll stick to women who can give out and get out. No more lovesick virgins."

She went scarlet. She couldn't even deny it. "I'll do my best to stay out of your way," she said.

"That would be appreciated," he replied. He couldn't look at her. It was hurting him to cut her up like this, but he had to make her angry enough to keep away from him. Wanting her was becoming an obsession that could cost him his job or his life under the right circumstances.

She dragged her eyes up for one brief instant. "Are you sorry we made love?" she asked huskily.

"Yes, I'm sorry," he said without a flicker of emotion. "I told you I'd been without a woman for a long time. You were handy, and you must know how beautiful you are." He forced a mocking smile. "It would have been a unique experience. I've never had a willing virgin before. But the newness would have worn off before morning, I'm afraid. I prefer an experienced woman in bed. Someone who knows how to play the game without expecting declarations of love and proposals of marriage."

Her face was very pale, but she smiled. "Well, no harm done," she said gamely. "Thanks for the instruction." She lowered her eyes to her coffee cup. "What time do you want to leave?"

He couldn't repress admiration for her bravery. No tears, no accusations, just acceptance despite her pain. That made it worse somehow. But he had to be strong.

He got up. "In half an hour," he said. "Leave the dishes. I'll be coming back here when I've put you on the plane."

"You aren't coming?" she exclaimed.

"No. I've got some leave due. I'm taking it now. I'll phone Eugene from the airport. Get your things together, please."

It was so hurried—the trip to the doctor's office, the antibiotic and tetanus shots, the rush to get to the airport in time to board a plane for Tulsa. She was en route before she realized how shocked and hurt she really was. It was a good thing that he hadn't let her say goodbye, so that she didn't break down. He'd given her the ticket, said something about having someone meet her at the airport, and then he'd left her at the right concourse gate without a goodbye or a backward glance.

She got off the plane in Tulsa and there was a car waiting. It whisked her back to her apartment. Once she got
into it, she threw herself on her bed and cried until her
eyes were red. But it didn't take away the sting of knowing that Hunter had only desired her. She'd given him
everything she had to give, and he'd still walked away
without a backward glance. She loved him more than her
own life. How was she going to live without him?

Ten

Jennifer couldn't decide what to do. She was so miserable that she only went through the motions of doing a job that she'd once loved. Her co-workers noticed the quiet pain in her face, but they were too kind to mention it.

Eugene got his molybdenum mine. The deal went through with flying colors, and the enemy agents went home in disgrace, having pursued the wrong site and gotten themselves in eternal hot water with their furious superiors.

Hunter stayed on vacation for a couple of weeks. When he came back into the office, he pointedly ignored Jennifer, refusing to even look her way when he passed her in the hall.

His attitude cut her to the bone. She lost weight and began to give in to nerves. She jumped when people approached unexpectedly. She made mistakes on her charts—the kind that she never would have made before.

Eugene called her on the carpet for her latest error, which had cost the company a good deal of money drilling in what turned out to be a dry hole.

"Everybody hits a dry hole once or twice," he raged at her in the privacy of his office. "And under normal circumstances, it's excusable. But, damn it, this isn't! This was carelessness, Jennifer, plain and simple."

"Yes, it was. And I'm going to turn in my resignation," she said, amazed to hear the words coming from her lips.

Apparently Eugene was, too, because he stopped in midtirade to scowl at her. His blue eyes narrowed and he studied her. After a minute, he leaned back in his chair with a long sigh.

"It's Hunter, of course," he said out loud, nodding at her shocked expression. "He tried to quit a couple of weeks ago, too. I refused his resignation and I'm refusing yours. You don't have to see each other. I've already made arrangements to transfer him to our Phoenix office for a few months. He leaves at the end of the week."

She didn't know what to say. It wasn't going to do any good to deny it. But it puzzled her that Hunter had offered to resign. She knew how much he loved his job.

"Surprises you that he tried to quit, doesn't it?" he asked her. "He wouldn't give a reason, but he keeps trying to get assignments out of the country. You, on the other hand, keep refusing any assignment that would require him to look after you. Interesting, isn't it?" He leaned forward abruptly. "What happened out on the desert? Did he make a pass?"

She lowered her eyes to the floor so they wouldn't give her away. "We had some differences of opinion," she replied. "And we agreed that it would be better if we kept out of each other's way in the future."

"Is that why you're losing weight and making one mistake on top of another?" he asked pleasantly.

She lifted her face proudly and stared him down. "I cost you a lot of money, so I guess you're entitled to know. I'm in love with him."

"How does he feel?"

"Mr. Hunter doesn't tell anyone how he feels," she replied. "He said point-blank that he doesn't want to get mixed up with a white woman in any emotional or physical way, and he told me to get lost."

Eugene whistled through his teeth. "Well!"

"I'm trying to get lost, except that I keep bumping into him and he stares right through me." Her voice revealed the pain of the experience all too well. She averted her face. "If you'll send him to Phoenix, I think I can get over him."

"Do you? I wouldn't make any bets on it. And if his temper is any indication, he's having some problems of his own. He was livid about letting you get shot. I gather that he feels responsible."

"It was my fault as much as his," she replied. "I don't blame him. My arm is as good as new."

"Too bad we can't say the same of your brain," Eugene mused. "It's a very good brain, too. I'll send him off. We'll see how you both feel in a few months. If this blows over, he can come back."

"Fair enough." She got to her feet. "Thank you."

"Have you tried talking to him?" he asked as she started to leave.

"He won't," she replied. "Once he makes up his mind, nobody gets a chance to change it."

"Just a thought," Eugene said with a smile. "It would be one way of finding out if he shares your feelings."

Jennifer tormented herself with that thought for the rest of the day. But it would do no good to throw herself at him again, she mused bitterly. He'd already shown her that he wanted her physically. It was every other way that he was rejecting her.

Still, she couldn't resist one last try. So when he came down the hall the morning before he was to leave for Phoenix, she deliberately stepped into his path.

"Eugene says you're being transferred," she said, clutching a stack of topo maps to her breasts to still the trembling of her hands.

Hunter looked down at her. She was wearing gray slacks with a white pullover knit blouse, her blond hair long and soft around her shoulders. He drank in the sight of her without letting her see that it was killing him to leave her.

"I'm going home for a few months, yes," he replied, staring down at her with no particular emotion in his dark face. "It's been a long time since I've had the opportunity to see my grandfather and my cousins and visit old friends."

She wondered if any of the old friends were female, but she didn't dare ask. She looked up into his eyes with her heart in her own, with no idea of how powerfully she was affecting him.

"I'll miss you," she said softly.

He lifted an eyebrow and smiled mockingly. "Will you? Why?"

She bit her lower lip without answering.

He stuck his hands into his pockets and the smile left his face as he looked down at her. "Sex is a bad basis for a relationship," he said bluntly. "I wanted you. Any man would. But common ground is something we never had, and never could. I don't want a white lover, any more than

I want a white wife. When I marry, if I marry, it will be to one of my own people. Is that clear enough?''

Her face went very pale, so that her blue eyes were the only color in it. "Yes," she said. "You told me that before."

"I want to make sure you get the message," he replied, forcing the words out. "It was a game. I play it with white women all the time. A little flirting, a little lovemaking, no harm done. But you're one of those throwbacks who equate sex with forever after. Sorry, honey, one night isn't worth my freedom, no matter how fascinating it was to have a virgin."

She dropped her wounded eyes to his sports jacket. "I see," she said, her voice haunted.

His fists clenched inside his pockets. It was killing him to do this! But he had to. He was so damned vulnerable that he wouldn't have the strength to resist her if she kept pursuing him. It had to end quickly. "Now go back to your office and stop trying to fan old flames. I've had all of you that I want. . . ."

She whirled and ran before he finished, tears staining her cheeks. Nothing had ever hurt so much. She went into her office and slammed the door, grateful that her co-workers were still at lunch. She dried her tears after a while and forced herself to work. But she knew she'd never forget the horrible things Hunter had said to her. So much for finding out how he really felt. He'd told her.

Hunter was on his way to the airport, feeling like an animal. Tears on that sweet, loving face had hurt him. It had taken every ounce of willpower he had not to chase her into the office and dry them. But he'd accomplished what he set out to do, he'd driven her away. Now all he had to do was live with it, and he'd never have to worry about the threat of Jennifer again.

Simple words. But as the weeks turned into months, he grew morose. Not seeing Jennifer was far worse than having her around. He missed her. His grandfather noticed his preoccupation and mentioned it to him one evening as they watched the horses prance in the corral.

"It is the white woman, is it not?" Grandfather Sanchez Owl asked in Apache.

"Yes," Hunter replied, too sad to prevaricate.

"Go to her," he was advised.

Hunter's hands tightened on the corral. "I cannot. She could never live here."

"If she loved you, she could." He touched the younger man's shoulder. "Your mother never loved your father. She found him unique and she collected him, as a man collects fine horses. When his uniqueness began to pale, she left him. It is the way of things. There was no love to begin with."

"You never told me this."

Grandfather's broad shoulders rose and fell. "It was not necessary. Now it is. This woman . . . she loves you?"

Hunter stared out over the corral. "She did. But I have done my best to make her hate me."

"Love is a gift. One should not throw it away."

Hunter glanced at him. "I thought that I could not give up my freedom. I thought that she, like my mother, would betray me."

"A man should think with his heart, not his head, when he loves," the old man said quietly. "You do love, do you not?"

Hunter looked away, wounded inside, aching as he thought of Jennifer's soft eyes promising heaven, remembered the feel of her chaste body in his arms, loving him. He closed his eyes. "Yes," he said huskily, fiercely. "Yes, I love!"

"Then go back before it is too late."

"She is white!" Hunter ground out.

The old man smiled. "So are you, in your thinking. It is something you do not want to face, but you are as comfortable in the white man's world as you are here. Probably more so, because your achievements are there and not here. A man can live with a foot in two worlds. You have proven it."

"It wouldn't be fair to a child," he said slowly.

The old man chuckled. "A man should have a son," he said. "Many sons. Many daughters. If they are loved, they will find a place in life. This white woman . . . is she handsome?"

Hunter saw her face as clearly as if she were standing beside him. "She is sunset on the desert," he said quietly. "The first bloom on the cactus. She is the silence of night and the beauty of dawn."

The old man's eyes grew misty with memory. "If she is all those things," he replied, "then you are a fool."

Hunter looked over at him. "Yes, I am." He moved away from the fence. "I am, indeed!"

He caught a plane that very afternoon. All the way to Tulsa, he prayed silently that he wasn't going to be too late. There was every chance that Jennifer had taken him seriously and found someone else. If she had, he didn't know how he was going to cope. He should have listened to his heart in the first place. If he'd lost her, he'd never forgive himself.

To say that Eugene was shocked to see him was an understatement. The old man sat at his desk and gaped when Hunter came into the office.

"I sent you to Phoenix," he said.

"I came back," Hunter returned curtly. "Jennifer isn't here. Where is she?"

Eugene's eyebrows arched. "Don't tell me you care, one way or the other?"

The dark face hardened visibly. "Where is she?"

"At her apartment, taking a well-earned vacation."

"I see."

Eugene narrowed one eye. "Before you get any ideas, she's been seeing one of the other geologists."

Hunter felt his breath stop in his throat. His dark eyes cut into Eugene's. "Has she?"

"Don't hurt her any more than you already have," the old man said, suddenly stern and as icy as his security chief had ever been. "She's just beginning to get over you. Leave her alone. Let her heal."

Something in Hunter wavered. He stared down at the carpeted floor, feeling uncertain for the first time in memory. "This geologist . . . is it serious?"

"I don't know. They've been dating for a couple of weeks. She's a little brighter than she has been, a little less brittle."

Hunter's hands clenched in his pockets. He looked up. "Is she well?" he asked huskily.

"She's better than she was just after you left," Eugene said noncommittally. He eyed the younger man quietly. "You've said often enough that you hated white woman. You finally convinced her. What do you want now—to torment her some more?"

Hunter averted his face and stared out the window. "My mother was white," he said after a minute, and felt rather than saw Eugene's surprise. "She walked out on my father when I was five. I thought she didn't love him enough to stay, but my grandfather said that she never loved him at all. It . . . made a difference in the way I looked at things. To ask a woman to marry a different culture, to accept a foreign way of life, is no small thing. But where love exists, perhaps hope does, too.''

Eugene softened. "You love her."

Hunter turned back to him. "Yes," he said simply. "Life without her is no life at all. Whatever the risk, it can't be as bad as the past few months have been."

The older man smiled. He picked up a sheaf of papers and tossed them across the desk. "There's your excuse. Tell her I sent those for her to look over."

Hunter took them, staring at the old man. "Have I killed what she felt?" he asked quietly. "Does she speak of me at all?"

Eugene sighed. "To be honest, no, she doesn't. Whatever her feelings, she keeps them to herself. I'm afraid I can't tell you anything. You'll have to go and find out for yourself."

He nodded. After a minute, he went out and closed the door quietly behind him. He wondered if Jennifer would even speak to him. Whether she'd be furiously angry or cold and unapproachable, remembering the brutal things he'd said to her when they parted.

All the way to her apartment, he refused to allow himself to think about it. But when he pressed the doorbell, he found that he was holding his breath.

Eleven

Jennifer left her dishes in the sink and went to answer the doorbell, a little irritated at the interruption. She'd spent the past few months in such misery that she was only beginning to get her head above water again. Missing Hunter had become a way of life, despite the fact that she'd started dating a very nice divorced geologist in her group. And if he did spend the whole of their evenings together talking about his ex-wife, what did that matter? Didn't she spend them talking about Hunter and things they'd done together?

She opened the door, and froze. So many lonely nights, dreaming of that hard, dark face, and here he stood. She felt her insides melting at just the sight of him, feeding on it like a starving woman.

She stared up at him with a helpless rapture in her eyes, the old warm vulnerability in her face. It had been so long since she'd seen him. The anguish of the time between lay

helplessly in her face as she looked at him. He watched her
with equal intensity. His dark eyes held hers for an endless, shattering moment before they slid down her thin
body and back up again. She looked as if she was shat-
tered to find him on her doorstep, but at least she wasn't
actively hostile. He measured her against his memories for
one long moment.

"You can't afford to lose this kind of weight," he said
softly. "Are you all right?"

His concern was almost her undoing. She had to fight
tears at the tenderness in his voice. She forced a smile.
Act, girl, she told herself. You can do it. You did it before, when it was even harder. He's surely here on business, so don't throw yourself at his feet.

"I've been on a diet," she lied. "Come in and I'll brew
some coffee. How are you?"

He stepped into the apartment, looking and feeling
alien in it. His eyes were restless, wandering around. Her
apartment reflected her personality and her life-style.
There were souvenirs from her travels everywhere, along
with the sunny colors that echoed her own personality,
and the numerous whimsical objects she delighted in.
Potted plants covered every inch of available space, and
ferns and green plants trailed down from high shelves.
There were Indian accents, too, including a war shield and
some basketry. His eyes lingered on those. Apache. He
smiled gently.

She saw where his gaze had fallen and tried to divert
him. "My dad says it looks like a jungle in here, but I like
green things," she said, leading him into the kitchen. She
tugged nervously at her yellow tank top. "How have you
been? Is this a business call? Did Eugene want me for
something? I'm just off for this week, but I guess . . . !"

"Eugene wanted me to drop some papers off for you," he said, drawing them out of his inside jacket pocket. He dropped them onto the kitchen table. "Something about a new rock formation one of your colleagues wants to check out." He pulled out a chair and straddled it, his eyes narrowing as he watched her make coffee. "I thought you might go back into the field after I left. What happened?"

"I've decided I like desk work," she said. It was a bald-faced lie, but he couldn't be told that. "I'm getting too old for fieldwork. Twenty-eight next birthday," she added with a smile.

"I know." He leaned his chin on his dark hands, clasped on the high back of the chair. "Still alone?" he pursued.

"There's a nice man in my office. Divorced, two kids. We . . . go out together." She glanced at him. "You?"

The geologist made him angry. Jealous. His dark eyes glittered and he found a weapon of his own. "There's a widow who lives next door to my grandfather, on the reservation. No kids. She's a great cook. No alarming habits."

"And she's Apache," she said for him on a bitter, painful laugh.

"Yes," he bit off. "She's Apache. No complications. No social barriers. No adjustments."

"Good for you. Going to marry her?"

He pulled out a cigarette and lit it without answering. The snub made her nervous.

She got down coffee cups and filled them. "Are you going to take off your coat, or is it glued on?"

He chuckled in spite of himself, shedding the expensive raincoat. She took it from him and carried it into the bedroom, to drape it carefully over the foot of her bed. A few minutes, that was all she had to get through. Then he'd go away, and she could again begin to try to get over him.

She went back into the kitchen, all smiles and courtesy and they talked about everything in the world except themselves. No matter what tactics he used to draw her out about her feelings, she parried them neatly. He was beginning to believe Eugene, that she had no feelings left for him. And he had only himself to blame, he knew. He'd deliberately tried to hurt her, to chase her away. The fact that his motives had been good ones at the time counted for nothing. He felt empty and alone. He knew he was going to feel that way for the rest of his life. He'd almost certainly lost her. She talked about the fellow geologist as though he'd become her world.

He put out his second cigarette and glanced at his watch. "I've got to go," he said in a voice without expression.

"Another overseas assignment, no doubt," she tried to sound cheery.

"Internal," he replied. He glanced at her. "I've given up fieldwork, too. I lost the taste for it."

That was surprising. He didn't seem the type to thrive on a desk job. But then, she'd thought she wasn't the type, either. She managed. Probably the widow didn't want him in a dangerous job anymore, and he'd given it up for her sake. The thought made her sick.

"I'll get your coat," she said, smiling. Her face would be frozen in its assumed position by the time he left, she thought ruefully.

She picked up his coat from the bed. This would be the last time. He'd marry the widow and she'd never see him again. She'd lost him for good now. She drew his coat slowly to her breasts and cradled it against her, tears clogging her eyes, her throat. She brought it to her lips and kissed it with breathless tenderness, bending her head over it with a kind of pain she'd never felt before in her life. It held the faint scent of the cologne he wore, of the tobacco he smoked. It smelled of him, and the touch of it was precious. She was losing him forever. She didn't know how she was going to live.

She straightened, feeling old and alone, wondering how she was going to go back in there and pretend that it didn't matter about his widow. That the past few months had been happy and full. That her life was fine without him in it.

In the other room, the man who'd happened to glance toward her bedroom had seen something reflected in the mirror facing the door that froze him where he stood. Her lighthearted act had convinced him that she didn't care, that she never had. But that woman holding his coat loved him. The emotion he saw in her face would haunt him forever, humble him every time he remembered the anguish in those soft blue eyes. She wasn't happy without him. He knew now that she'd been pretending ever since he'd walked into the apartment. She'd only been putting on an act about not caring, to hide her real feelings. He grimaced, thinking how close a call it had been. If he'd taken her act for granted and left, his life would never have been the same.

He caught his breath and turned away. All his former arguments about the reasons they were better apart vanished in an agony of need. If he walked out that door, she was going to die. If not physically, surely emotionally. She loved him that much. He loved her that much, too. It was vaguely frightening, to love to that degree. But even with the obstacles, they were going to make it. He'd never been more certain of anything in his life.

He took the coat from her when she rejoined him, her mask firmly in place again. She couldn't know that he'd seen her through the mirror, so he didn't let on. He wanted to see how far she was willing to go with the charade, if she could keep it up until he walked out. Now that he knew how she felt, it was like anticipating a Christmas present that was desperately wanted.

"It was nice to see you again," she said as she went with him to the door.

"Same here." He opened the door and stood silhouetted in it, with his long back to her, looking alien and somehow unapproachable. "You haven't said whether you were glad to see me, Jennifer," he said quietly, without turning.

She lowered her eyes to the floor. "It's always good to see old . . . friends, Phillip."

He drew in his breath sharply. The sound of his name in her soft voice brought back unbearable memories. "Were we ever friends?"

"No. Not really. I'm . . . I'm glad . . . about your widow, I mean," she said, unable to conceal a faint note of bitter anguish in her tone.

He sighed, still with his back to her. "The widow just turned eighty-two. She's my godmother."

Her heart jumped. She took a steadying breath. "The divorced man only takes me out so he can talk about his ex-wife. He still loves her."

He turned. He shook his head, the light in his eyes disturbing, humbling. "Oh, God, what a close call we had! You little idiot, do you really think I came here on business?" He held out his arms and she went into them. And just that quickly, that easily, the obstacles were pushed aside, the loneliness of the past gone forever.

He bent to her mouth and hers answered it. She moaned, shuddering, her control gone forever.

He lifted his head, and had to fight her clinging arms. "I'm going to close and lock the door, that's all," he whispered shakily, reaching out to do it. "I don't want the neighbors to watch us make love."

"Are we going to?" she asked helplessly.

He nodded. "Oh, yes," he said fervently. He bent, lifting her in his arms. "I love you," he whispered at her lips, watching the soft, incredulous wonder grow in her face as he said it. "And now I'm going to prove it physically, in the intimacy of lovemaking. At least I won't have to hurt you, will I, little one?" he asked, smiling gently at the memory of that night in his house.

She clung to him, shivering helplessly, her face buried in the heated skin of his throat. "You won't give me a child, ever, will you?" she whimpered.

His breath caught. He paused at the bedroom door, meeting her sad, hungry eyes. He started to speak, failed. He looked down at her mouth. "I won't . . . use anything, if you like," he whispered. His eyes went back up to hers, lost in their shocked delight. "It's all right," he said, his voice tender. "A child . . . will be all right."

She was crying. He undressed her gently, but she couldn't even see him through her tears. She loved him. He loved her. There would be children and years of being together, wherever they chose to live. On the reservation, off it, in the desert, anywhere at all.

She said so, seeing him come down on the bed beside her, a blur of mahogany skin and lean muscle.

"Say the words while I'm loving you," he whispered, his lips slow and tender on her yielded body.

"The . . . words?" she echoed, arching as his mouth pressed down on her flat belly.

"That you love me," he said lazily. "I said it, but you didn't."

"How could you not know?" she moaned achingly. "I offered myself every time you looked at me. I did everything but wear a button.... Oh!" She stiffened as his mouth touched her in an unexpected way.

He lifted his head, his eyes darkly smoldering. "Do you want that?" he whispered.

She almost didn't answer him. She had a feeling that the experienced women he'd known had expected it, and an equally strong feeling that it was something he'd do for her sake, but never for his own.

She sat up, touching his lean face lovingly. "If you want it," she whispered. "I . . ." Her eyes fell to his chest, and further. She caught her breath at the sight of him. "I'll do anything you want me to."

He tilted her eyes back up to his. "Is it something you want?"

She shook her head. "I'm sorry . . ."

"Sorry!" He laughed with soft delight and caught her close, his mouth rough on her bare shoulder. "I'm as old-fashioned as you are, in some ways. Not really modern enough for this day and age. But if you want that kind of intimacy, you can have it."

"Maybe someday," she whispered. "When I'm less inhibited." She flushed. "Right now, all of it is a little scary . . ."

He lifted his head and his dark eyes searched hers. "We'll sit up this time, and you can control when it happens."

She went scarlet. He brushed her mouth with his. "Don't be shy," he whispered into her lips. "It's as new to me as it is to you, to make love and be in love. I don't want to make it disappointing for you."

"It could never be that," she said gently. "Not with you."

"Try to remember that it's an art, like any other," he said, brushing back her hair. "It isn't perfection at first. It may be uncomfortable despite what we did in my bed that night, and there may not be much pleasure in it for you. I can make it up to you afterward." He drew in a slow breath. "I've been without a woman for a long time, and my body isn't always mine to control. I'll hold back as long as I can...."

His anguish made her feel protective. She lifted her lips to his face and kissed his eyes closed, loving the newness of being in love, of being loved in return, of being wanted. "Whatever you do to me will be all right," she whispered. "Love me, now, please. Teach me."

"God, what a thing to tempt a man with," he groaned. He eased her down on the bed, and his mouth found her with aching expertness. He kissed and touched and teased until the flames were blazing in her slender body, until she was crying and twisting up to his mouth and hurting with her need of him.

She was only dimly aware when he moved, sitting back against the headboard with her body over his. He lifted her, his hands faintly tremulous, and positioned her so that she felt him suddenly in stark, hot intimacy.

Her eyes dilated, looking straight into his. He took her hands and placed them on his hips.

"Now," he whispered.

She hesitated, but the strain in his face made her realize the torment he was enduring for her sake. She bit her lower lip and pushed. To her amazement, there was only a little discomfort, but not pain. She gasped.

He smiled gently, even through his excitement. "Yes," he whispered. "I thought it might be so. There's nothing to be afraid of now."

His hands settled, warm and hard on her hips. He whispered to her, something that made her body shiver, something so intimate that she gasped and her blood surged in her veins. And at that moment, his hands jerked mercilessly and she felt the white-hot fury of sudden pleasure biting into her.

He rolled over with her, still a part of her body, his voice whispering, coaxing. His mouth brushed against hers, his lips tender, his hands touching her. His mouth settled gently on hers and he began to move, very slowly.

She jerked helplessly. "Phillip!" she exclaimed as the sudden pleasure made her rigid.

"Hold on," he murmured against her mouth. "I'm going to make you want me so badly that you'll fly in my arms. Bite me. That's it, bite me!" he whispered fiercely.

She'd dreamed of a tender, slow initiation with moonbeams and pink clouds. Instead, it was like a vicious fever with pleasure so throbbing and fierce and merciless that she became wanton.

Her nails bit into him, like her teeth. He pushed her down into the mattress with the rough thrust of his body and she arched up to receive it, her legs tangling in his. She looked up at him, her eyes fastened to his, her breath gasping out as his face moved closer and then away, and the mattress rose and fell noisily.

"Look down," he said under his breath.

She did, too lost in him to be shy anymore. He looked, too, and when her eyes met his, passion was smoldering in them.

"Show me where, Jennifer," he whispered, moving her hands to his hips. "Teach me where you feel the most pleasure when I move."

She flushed, but she obeyed him, guided his body, and cried out when he followed her lead. And then it all seemed to explode at once. His movements were rough and quick, his powerful body strong enough for both of them, his hands controlling her wild thrashing, holding her down, making her submit. His mouth crushed into hers and she heard his tortured breathing, his harsh groans, as the pleasure arched him into her body.

Incredibly she went with him. Soaring. Up into the sun. Shivering with cold and heat so intricately mingled that she was only living as part of him. She was saying something, but she couldn't hear her own voice.

When she opened her eyes again, there was a new kind of lassitude in her limbs. They felt numb and boneless, like the rest of her body. She could breathe again. Her heartbeat was almost normal.

A dark, loving pair of eyes came into view above her. "That," he whispered, "is the sweetest expression of love I'll ever experience in my life. You're my woman."

"Yes." She said it with shy pride, because now it was over. The mystery was gone, but the magic remained. She touched his mouth, fascinated. "Will I get pregnant from it?" she whispered.

He smiled lazily. "I hope so," he whispered. "Creation should be like this, from seed so exquisitely planted in love. Now do you understand what I meant, about not making a casual entertainment out of something so profound? The ultimate glory of lovemaking is the act of creation." He bent and kissed her with rapt tenderness. "I want to plant my seed in you. If we can make a baby together, even if he is a product of two worlds, I want to."

She clung to him, her mouth ardent and loving. "So do I," she whispered huskily. "Oh, so do I! I love you."

"I love you just as much," he said with fierce possession. He was surprised at how quickly his body responded when he kissed her, at the kindling passion that bound them together almost at once.

"No, don't stop," she whispered when he hesitated.

"It's too soon..."

"No!" She pulled him down to her and put her mouth hungrily against his and felt him shudder. She opened her eyes as his body slid over hers and they melted together with delicious ease.

"You see?" she whispered shakily. "It's so easy now."

"So easy." He smiled tenderly and his mouth bent to hers. He bit at it, very gently, and his body echoed that tenderness, his arms enfolding hers. He rolled abruptly onto his side and smiled at her surprise. "That night in Washington, I wanted to do it like this, remember? Now we can. Put this leg over mine, here," he guided softly. "Now, like this...!"

She watched his face contort as his hand brought her hips suddenly against his. It was fascinating to watch him, to see the passion kindle and ignite.

"Jennifer, you're staring," he whispered.

"I know. I want to watch you," she whispered back, her eyes wide and soft and curious. "Is it all right if I look?"

He shuddered. Her fascination with his pleasure brought it all too soon. His body buckled and began to shudder. He felt the familiar tension building to flashpoint, hamstringing him, racking him. He looked into her eyes and felt her hands shyly tugging at his hips and he cried out.

Convulsions of unbearable pleasure ripped through him. He was aware at some level of her stare, of her scarlet face as she saw him experience fulfillment. It made it all the more shattering. He was helpless and she was seeing him this way, but it didn't matter. Nothing mattered. He was burning. Burning. Burning!

He cried out, his body rippling beside hers. She pressed into his arms and helped him, loving the fury of his hands gripping her hips, loving the unbridled pleasure she saw in his face. He was truly hers, now. Completely hers. She shivered, amazed that his own satisfaction caused her body to fulfill itself in one long, hot wave of shuddering pleasure.

Long afterward, they slept. When she woke at last, it was to the smell of something delicious cooking in the kitchen. She got up and dressed, slowly, with the memory of what had happened like a candle in her mind.

Phillip was standing at the stove cooking steak. He was wearing only the trousers from his suit. His chest and feet were bare. He glanced up as she joined him, and his eyes were warm and tender.

"Are you hungry?" he asked, opening one arm to draw her to him and kiss her softly.

"A little," she whispered. Her eyes met his. "Do you really love me?"

"With all my heart," he whispered back, his eyes punctuating the words. "Life without you is no life, Jennifer. You'll have to get used to having an Apache husband."

"You want to marry me?" she asked, holding her breath.

He put down the fork he was using to turn the steak and brought her against him, bending to kiss her with fierce hunger. "Of course I want to marry you!" he said impatiently, when he lifted his head. "I always did. But the memory of how it was for my mother colored my whole life. Until my grandfather told me the truth—that my father was only a conversation piece for her; that she never loved him. He sent me to you," he added huskily. "He said that I was a fool."

She smiled gently. "No. Just a man afraid to trust. But I'll never hurt you, my darling," she said, sliding her arms around him, laying her blond head on his bare chest. "I'll give you children and live with you anywhere you say."

"Your job..." he began.

"Geology isn't something you forget. I'll have babies for a few years, then when they're in school, I'll work out of the Tucson or Phoenix offices. Eugene won't fire me completely."

His lean hands stilled on her back. "I can't let you make that kind of sacrifice for me."

She lifted her head. "You gave up fieldwork," she replied. "And I know how much you loved it. You did that because of me, didn't you?"

"Yes," he admitted finally. "I didn't want the risk. I was thinking about how it would be for you and the children while I was away."

She smiled with pure delight. "Me and the children," she mused. "And yet you went away swearing that you wanted nothing to do with me."

"Lying through my teeth," he added with a dry chuckle. "I drove my grandfather crazy."

She reached up and touched his thick, dark eyebrows. "We're so different in coloring. I wonder if our children will look like you or me?"

"I hope they'll look like both of us," he replied. "My grandfather said that I was living proof that a man can have a foot in two worlds." He smiled at her. "He doesn't like whites, as a rule, but he'll like you."

"My parents will like you," she returned.

He frowned. "Are you sure?"

"Well, I did just happen to tell them about you a few thousand times over the past few years, and I had this picture that I begged out of the personnel files. My mother thought you were striking, and my father was sure you'd be able to keep me out of dangerous places if I ever married you."

"They don't mind the cultural differences?" he stressed.

"They raised me with a mind of my own and let me use it," she replied. "They're not rigid people, as you'll see when you meet them. They're very educated people with tolerant personalities. Besides all that, they want grand-children."

"I see. That was the selling point, was it?" he murmured.

"Yes, it was. So we'd better set a date and get busy."

He bent and kissed her, ignoring the smell of burning steak. "How does next Friday suit you?" he asked.

"Just fine." She kissed him back, smiling. The steak went right on burning, and nobody noticed until it was the color of tar and the texture of old leather. Which was just as well, because they were in too much of a hurry to get to the courthouse for a marriage license to worry about food, anyway.

*   *   *   *   *

SILHOUETTE® Desire™

COMING NEXT MONTH

#607 GLORY, GLORY—Linda Lael Miller
Years ago, Glory Parsons had been forced to flee her hometown—and Jesse Bainbridge. Now she's returned with shocking news about his adopted niece. Could Jesse ever forgive Glory's special secret?

#608 LOOKING FOR TROUBLE—Nancy Martin
Police officer Sheila Malone knew Max Bollinger spelled *trouble*. She thought the sexy aristocrat was innocent of murder, but proving it would've been easier if he hadn't also stolen her heart!

#609 THE BRIDAL PRICE—Barbara Boswell
Marry without love? Never! But cool, sophisticated Carling Templeton did just that to protect her father... never expecting arrogant rancher Kane McClellan to be the man of her dreams.

#610 UPON A MIDNIGHT CLEAR—Laura Leone
Bah humbug! That's how Fiona Larkin felt at Christmastime. But when mischief at her pet motel called for the help of security consultant Eli Becker, Fiona discovered a season of love.

#611 THE PENDRAGON VIRUS—Cait London
When *Ms.* Dallas Pendragon bet macho bachelor Sam Loring that he'd fail trying to act as a working mother for a month, he expected to win—more than the wager....

#612 HANDSOME DEVIL—Joan Hohl
Selena McInnes was undaunted and unimpressed by strong men, until she met December's *Man of the Month*, handsome devil Luke Branson, in this passionate sequel to *The Gentleman Insists*.

AVAILABLE NOW:

WRITTEN IN THE STARS

Star-crossed lovers?
Or a match made in heaven?

Why are some heroes strong and silent . . . and others charming and cheerful? The answer is WRITTEN IN THE STARS!

Coming each month in 1991, Silhouette Romance presents you with a special love story written by one of your favorite authors—highlighting the hero's astrological sign! From January's sensible Capricorn to December's disarming Sagittarius, you'll meet a dozen dazzling and distinct heroes.

Twelve heavenly heroes . . . twelve wonderful Silhouette Romances destined to delight you. Look for one WRITTEN IN THE STARS title every month throughout 1991—only from Silhouette Romance.

STAR

Silhouette Books ®

Take 4 bestselling love stories FREE
Plus get a FREE surprise gift!

From *New York Times* Bestselling author
Penny Jordan, a compelling novel of ruthless passion
that will mesmerize readers everywhere!

Penny Jordan

Silver

Real power, true power came from
Rothwell. And Charles vowed to have it,
the earldom and all that went with it.

Silver vowed to destroy Charles, just as surely and
uncaringly as he had destroyed her father; just as he had
intended to destroy her. She needed him to want her . . .
to desire her . . . until he'd do anything to have her.

But first she needed a tutor: a man who wanted no one.
He would help her bait the trap.

**Played out on a glittering international stage,
Silver's story leads her from the luxurious comfort of
British aristocracy into the depths of adventure,
passion and danger.**

AVAILABLE NOW!

 HARLEQUIN

Win 1 of 10 Romantic Vacations and Earn Valuable Travel Coupons Worth up to $1,000!

Inside every Harlequin or Silhouette book during September, October and November, you will find a PASSPORT TO ROMANCE that could take you around the world.

By sending us the official entry form available at your favorite retail store, you will automatically be entered in the PASSPORT TO ROMANCE sweepstakes, which could win you a star-studded London Show Tour, a Carribean Cruise, a fabulous tour of France, a sun-drenched visit to Hawaii, a Mediterranean Cruise or a wander through Britain's historical castles. The more entry forms you send in, the better your chances of winning!

In addition to your chances of winning a fabulous vacation for two, valuable travel discounts on hotels, cruises, car rentals and restaurants can be yours by submitting an offer certificate (available at retail stores) properly completed with proofs-of-purchase from any specially marked PASSPORT TO ROMANCE Harlequin® or Silhouette® book. The more proofs-of-purchase you collect, the higher the value of travel coupons received!

For details on your PASSPORT TO ROMANCE, look for information at your favorite retail store or send a self-addressed stamped envelope to:

PASSPORT TO ROMANCE
P.O. Box 621
Fort Erie, Ontario L2A 5X3

ONE PROOF-OF-PURCHASE

3-CSD-3

To collect your free coupon booklet you must include the necessary number of proofs-of-purchase with a properly completed offer certificate available in retail stores or from the above address.

© 1990 Harlequin Enterprises Limited